Books by April Wilson

**McIntyre Security
Bodyguard Series:**

Vulnerable

Fearless

Shane (a novella)

Broken

Shattered

Imperfect

Ruined

Hostage

Redeemed

Marry Me (a novella)

Snowbound (a novella)

Regret

With This Ring (a novella)

Collateral Damage

Special Delivery

**McIntyre Security
Protectors:**

Finding Layla

**McIntyre Security
Search and Rescue Series:**

Search and Rescue

Lost and Found

A Tyler Jamison Novel:

Somebody to Love

Somebody to Hold

Somebody to Cherish

**A British Billionaire
Romance:**

Charmed (co-written with
Laura Riley)

**Audiobooks & Upcoming
Releases:**

For links to my audiobooks
and upcoming releases,
visit my website:

www.aprilwilsonauthor.com

Somebody to Cherish

A Tyler Jamison Novel

Book 3

by

April Wilson

Copyright © 2022 April E. Barnswell/
Wilson Publishing LLC
All rights reserved.

Cover by Steamy Designs
Photography by Jeanne Woodfin Photography
Model: Daniel Rengering
Proofreading by Amanda Cuff (Word of Advice)

Published by
April E. Barnswell
Wilson Publishing LLC
P.O. Box 292913
Dayton, OH 45429
www.aprilwilsonauthor.com

ISBN: 9798829395599

No part of this publication may be reproduced, stored in a
retrieval system, copied, shared, or transmitted in any form
or by any means without the prior written permission of the
author. The only exception is brief quotations to be used in book
reviews. Please don't steal e-books.

This novel is entirely a work of fiction. All places and locations
are used fictitiously. The names of characters and places are
figments of the author's imagination, and any resemblance to real
people or real places is purely coincidental and unintended.

Character List

- Tyler Jamison – 45 yrs old, former Chicago homicide detective, now a private investigator
- Ian Alexander – 28 yrs old, independently wealthy, now a private investigator
- Layla Alexander – 21 yrs old, university student, Ian's sister
- Jason Miller – 28 yrs old, Layla's boyfriend and bodyguard
- Judge Martin Alexander – Ian's father and federal judge
- Ruth Alexander – Ian's mother and district attorney
- Brad Turner – a 40-something year old man who physically assaulted Ian in a previous book, and who fought with Tyler leading to charges against Tyler
- Beth McIntyre – 25 yrs old, Tyler's younger sister, she's married to Shane
- Shane McIntyre – 37 yrs old, Tyler's brother-in-law, married to Beth
- Liam McIntyre – 24 yrs old, Shane's youngest brother, martial arts expert and instructor
- Sam Harrison – 30 yrs old, Ian's friend, Cooper's partner, Beth's best friend and bodyguard
- Cooper – 56 yrs old, Sam's partner, Shane's best friend and business partner

- Rachel Harrison – 32 yrs old, a nurse, Sam's sister visiting from Dayton, OH
- Ingrid Jamison – 64 yrs old, Tyler's widowed mother
- Joe Rucker – 58 yrs old, African-American former heavyweight boxer, Beth's chauffeur

ꮯ 1

Tyler Jamison

I'm enjoying this way too much. Watching Ian on the mat with Liam McIntyre is entertaining as hell. This is Ian's third private self-defense class in a week. Even though Liam's taking it easy on his student, it's not looking good for Ian, who's spending most of his time flat on his ass. I have to give Ian credit, though. He's taking his new role as a private investigator seriously, and he's holding up his end of the bargain by getting self-defense training.

My two requirements for Ian, if he wanted to join me in my new venture as a private investigator, were that he take self-defense classes and learn how to safely handle a gun. He's currently working on both of those tasks. In fact, he's giving it his all.

It's not like he ever has to work a day in his life. He doesn't. Ian inherited an impressive fortune from his paternal grandfather, and his net worth puts him near the top of just about any *Forbes* list you can think of. But he wants this. He wants a career—and he wants to work with me.

As for my take on the situation, I'm deeply touched that he's determined to join me in my new venture, but I have to admit I'm worried that he could get hurt in the process. Hence, my two requirements.

The bleachers shake as Shane steps up and sits beside me. "How's he doing?" There's a hint of amusement in his voice.

Shane McIntyre, my brother-in-law and the CEO of McIntyre Security, is dressed in his typical work attire—a charcoal gray suit and tie, a white dress shirt, and polished black loafers. There's a shiny silver Rolex on his wrist. Shane's probably the only one in the building who's wearing a suit—it's a visual reminder that he's the one in charge here. Not that anyone needs reminding.

I, on the other hand, am dressed in blue jeans and a T-shirt—a far cry from what I used to wear when I was a Chicago homicide detective. *Was.* I'm still trying to get used to thinking of my twenty-year career in law enforcement in the past tense. Those days are behind me now. I was fired for violating the conditions of my administrative leave. I wouldn't change a thing, though. I gladly broke the rules in order to save the life of Ian's younger sister, Layla.

Shane was kind enough to lend us his youngest brother, Liam, who's a martial arts expert. Liam teaches both martial arts and self-defense classes to McIntyre Security employees and clients. Today, Ian's getting a private lesson courtesy of Shane. It's a personal favor for his wife's brother—that would be me.

"It's not going very well at the moment," I admit, finally getting around to answering his question. "But I'm sure he'll get the hang of it eventually."

I flinch when Ian hits the mat once again.

Laughing good-naturedly, Liam offers his hand to Ian and pulls him up onto his feet. Once upright, Ian dusts himself off, wincing when his hands brush his backside. I'm sure he's bruised, the poor guy. He'll definitely need some TLC tonight.

And I look forward to giving it to him.

"He's got to start somewhere," Shane says. "If he's going to work with you, he needs to know how to protect himself. You never know when a situation will go south."

After losing my career in law enforcement, I decided to get my private investigator's license. Just because I'm no longer a cop doesn't mean I have to stop helping people. Rescuing Layla from a sex trafficking ring proved that to me. Instead of investigating murders, I will now hopefully get the chance to prevent some.

And Ian's decided he's going to join me in my new venture. Honestly, I'm not sure how I feel about it. The idea of my boyfriend in harm's way doesn't sit well with me. Ian has no physical combat experience, no weapons training. That means he's got a lot to learn. And I have to figure out how to deal with the idea of him possibly getting hurt.

Ian's dressed in a pair of gray workout shorts and a black tank top. His curly brown hair is matted with sweat, and those eager green eyes of his keep sliding over to me. I think he's still gloating that I agreed to let him join me.

I'm pretty sure I'm going to regret that decision the first time Ian gets hurt.

Right now, Liam's teaching Ian how to escape from a rear choke hold. Ian struggles as he tries to pivot and break free of Liam's grip.

Shane pats me on the back. "Give him time. He'll get the hang of it." He pauses a moment. "Any word from Brad Turner?"

"No, nothing. Hopefully it will stay that way. He's given us enough grief as it is. Ian doesn't need more of Turner's crap."

Brad Turner—he's the reason I lost my job with the Chicago police department. He filed charges against me when I beat him up in the bathroom at a local nightclub, Sapphires. Hell, he deserved everything he got. I found him pinning Ian to the cement block wall, choking him. At the sight of Ian's bottom lip, swollen and bleeding, I lost control and pummeled Turner. It took two club security guards to haul me off of him.

Turner reported the incident to the police, conveniently leaving out the part where he physically assaulted Ian. At first, I was looking at felony charges because of the level of damage I did to his face—charges that would have resulted in a mandatory prison sentence for me.

But ultimately, my attorney, Troy Spencer, managed to get a plea deal for me. In exchange for pleading guilty, I was charged with a misdemeanor instead, which meant a short visit to the county jail instead of a lengthy prison sentence.

Shane stands. "Good. I hope Turner keeps quiet. If he becomes a problem, let me know. I'll have Dominic talk to him."

I chuckle at the idea of Dominic Zaretti talking to Brad Turner. That's a euphemism if I ever heard one. Dominic has a tendency to talk with his fists, and as he's a freaking huge giant of a man, those fists are capable of doing a lot of damage. "I'll keep that in mind. Thanks."

"I'm off to a meeting," Shane says. "Before I forget, Beth wanted me to invite you guys over for dinner tomorrow night. Your niece and nephew need some uncle time. Your mom's coming, too."

Distracted, I nod, my focus returning to Ian. "We wouldn't miss it for the world."

"I'll see you then." Shane walks down the bleacher steps and exits the martial arts studio.

Liam walks Ian through the steps of escaping a rear choke hold one more time. This time, Ian manages to elbow Liam and twist his body at the right moment, breaking free of Liam's grasp.

I'm pretty sure Liam let Ian have that little win.

When the hour-long session is over, Liam disappears into his office, and Ian jogs over to me. "So, whatcha think?" he asks breathlessly.

I'm debating whether to be honest with him or go gentle. I opt for gentle. Ian's trying so hard, I don't want to discourage him. He's a lover, a dancer—not a fighter. But still, he's trying. "Nice improvement today, baby."

Ian laughs, his green eyes twinkling with amusement. "Liar." He nods toward the locker room. "I'm going to grab a quick shower and change my clothes." He sniffs his arm pit and scowls. "Man, I reek. I won't be long."

While Ian's showering, I stick my head into Liam's office. "So, how'd he do?"

Liam smiles. "He's doing better."

"You should see him on the dance floor. The guy's got moves. It's not that he's uncoordinated."

"It just takes practice," Liam says. "Lots and lots of practice. He'll get the hang of it, I promise."

"Thanks for everything you're doing for him. I really appreciate it."

I head to the locker room, which we have all to ourselves. I arrive just as Ian steps out of a shower stall with a white towel wrapped around his lean waist. He has a dancer's body, toned and agile. And there's not an ounce of fat on him. We're the same height—both of us six feet tall—but I outweigh him by a good twenty pounds of solid muscle.

He spots me as he finger-combs the longer strands of curls on the top of his head. The sides are trimmed short, an undercut. "Just give me a second to get dressed, and we can get out of here."

"How do you feel?"

Flexing his shoulders and arms, he winces. "Not too bad. I might have bruised my ass, though."

"I think you bruised more than just your ass." I laugh. "Don't worry. I'll be gentle with you. How about a back rub when we get home?"

He grins. "That sounds wonderful."

I study Ian as he dries off. He knows perfectly well I'm watching. He drops the towel where he stands, giving me a clear view of his naked body. *Damn.* Every inch of him is perfection. He has a lean, lightly-muscled build. A light dusting of brown hair on his chest narrows into a thin line that bisects his abs. His nipple piercings catch my eye.

Ian smiles knowingly at me as he pulls on a pair of teal

briefs—his signature color. "Do you like what you see, detective?"

I chuckle. We both know I'm no longer a detective, but the title has stuck.

My heartrate shoots up when Ian steps into a pair of ripped skinny jeans. He shimmies as he pulls them up and fastens them.

He slips on a teal T-shirt that hugs his torso and biceps. "Yeah, you do," Ian says as he slides his feet into a pair of worn sneakers. He reaches around to cup his ass. "Admit it. You want some of this."

"Yeah, we'll see about that," I say, smiling as I follow him out of the locker room. When I lightly smack his ass, he winces. "Something tells me you won't be sitting for a while."

Just as we're leaving the locker room, the next class of students starts arriving. It's a mixed group of men and women, mostly McIntyre Security clients who are here for a self-defense class. We wave goodbye to Liam as we head for the exit.

Once we're out in the hallway, away from curious eyes, I cup the back of Ian's head and draw him close. "You did good today."

His eyes lock on mine. "Admit it. I sucked."

I can't help smiling. "You'll get the hang of it." And then I lean in and press my lips to his. When I pull back, his lips cling to mine for a moment before he breaks away.

I slide my hand down to grip the back of his neck—something I know he likes. "We've been invited to dinner tomorrow night at the penthouse."

He smiles. "Cool. Will Ingrid be there, too?"

Ian and my mom have developed a very interesting friendship. She's been teaching him to cook my favorite childhood dishes, and now they're sharing recipes. Luckily for me, Ian loves to cook. Back in my bachelor days, I subsisted almost solely on take-out and frozen dinners. Ian doesn't mind carry-out, but he refuses to let me eat anything that comes from a box in the freezer. "Yes, my mother will be there."

He nods as we head toward the elevator. "Excellent."

ↁ **2**

Tyler Jamison

When we arrive home, I park in the driveway, and we walk up to the carriage house. After I decided to go into business for myself, we converted the old carriage house on Ian's property into the offices of Jamison Investigations.

After Ian and I recently passed our private investigator licensing exams, we opened for business. So far, we've had two relatively simple cases.

The two-story structure across the drive from the

townhouse has four main rooms on the ground floor—the front office, where our admin, Kimi, monitors the phones and e-mail; our shared private office; Jerry's office; and a small conference room where we can meet with clients. There's also a small employee lounge for the four of us and a storage room about the size of a closet.

We converted the second floor into an apartment for Jerry Harshman, our assistant and all-around handyman. Jerry was a homeless veteran when Ian met him. He lived on the streets, and Ian helped him out occasionally by buying him hot meals. Ian had tried for several years to get Jerry into a shelter, but the man refused. After we decided to start our PI business, Ian offered Jerry a job, and he gladly took it. Lucky for us, the man has some serious skills.

Jerry's in his late sixties, tall and sturdy, with a deep baritone voice. His silver hair is buzzed short, his skin weathered and lined, his eyes a steely blue. Back in the day, he was a staff sergeant in the Army. Today, he does a number of tasks for us, everything from ordering office supplies to organizing deliveries. We even had him conducting surveillance on one of our first cases.

Kimi started out as a temporary employee, but she fit so well we offered her a full-time job. She adds a lot of color to the office—literally—with her short, spikey purple hair, numerous facial piercings, and colorful tattoos. We liked her immediately. Her energy is infectious.

When we walk into the office, Kimi waves a note in the air. "Perfect timing, bitches." She grins, displaying dimples. "It looks like we might have a new case. Someone named Gina Capelli called. She said she's a friend of Beth McIntyre's and that she needs your help."

I'm sure I look as surprised as I feel. I know Gina Capelli well. Her brother, Peter, is the owner of Renaldo's, a five-star Italian restaurant on N. Michigan. He's a big deal in this town. He also happens to be a close friend of Shane's. Gina owns a popular café in downtown Chicago on Superior Street, not too far from where we live.

Ian snatches the note from Kimi's hand. He reads it, then hands it to me.

Some lady named Gina Capelli called. She said someone's stealing from her coffee shop. Beth suggested she ask us for help.

"Do you want me to call her?" Kimi asks.

Just as I nod, Jerry walks into the front room holding a clipboard and a pen. "The conference room furniture will arrive Friday," he says in a gruff voice. He looks to Ian, then to me. "So, how did the self-defense class go?"

"It went well," I say.

Ian laughs. "He's just being nice. I sucked, again. And thanks for ordering the furniture, Jerry."

"No problem, son," Jerry says.

Kimi walks around her desk and hands me a cordless phone. "Here she is. Gina Capelli."

I take the phone. "Hello, Gina. It's Tyler. I understand you need some help."

"Tyler! It's so good to hear your voice. Yes, I need help. Someone is stealing cash out of my back office at the café. I don't want to involve the police, so I need someone to figure out who's doing this. Can you help?"

"I'm sure we can. When's a good time for us to meet? We can come to you."

"Are you free this afternoon? Maybe around two?"

"That sounds fine. We'll see you then." After I end the call and hand the phone back to Kimi, I tell Ian, "Two o'clock."

Since we have some time to kill, Ian and I head across the driveway and enter the townhouse through the back door, which leads right into the kitchen.

Ian heads to the sink to wash his hands. "I'm starving. I'll make us some lunch."

Ian grew up in a household with its own private

French chef—recruited from Paris, by Ian's parents—so he's picked up more than a few culinary skills over the years. I, on the other hand, am limited to what I can cook on a gas grill.

Ian dries his hands on a kitchen towel. "We don't have much time, so I'll just whip up some grilled chicken wraps using last night's leftovers. They'll go great with the fresh hummus I made."

I sit at the kitchen island and watch him work. "You seem to be moving all right," I note. "You don't seem sore."

He laughs as he pulls the chicken out of the fridge and sets it on the counter. "Just don't expect me to sit down anytime soon." He reaches around to cup his ass through his jeans and groans dramatically.

"Sounds to me like you're angling for some TLC tonight."

He smiles. "That would not be amiss. Maybe a gentle massage? Perhaps some well-placed kisses?"

While he assembles our lunch, I set out plates and silverware. When it's just the two of us, we prefer to eat at the island counter. I grab some potato chips and pull two Cokes out of the fridge.

Ian sets a plate in front of me. "So, if someone's stealing from the coffee shop, why doesn't Gina just call the police? It's not that I don't appreciate the call, but if someone's robbing her, surely she should let the cops handle it."

"We'll find out soon enough." I take a sip of my Coke. "My guess is, she's afraid it's one of her employees taking the money, and she doesn't want to get them in trouble."

"That would suck." Ian takes a bite of his wrap. "Mm, this homemade hummus is divine. D'you like it? Your mom gave me the recipe."

"I think it's cute you and my mom have bonded."

Ian shrugs. "She tells me stories about when you were a kid. Ingrid's amazing."

Once we're done eating, we run upstairs to get ready for our meeting with Gina. We need to change into something a bit more professional.

While I'm sitting on the side of the bed putting on my shoes, Ian walks out of the closet wearing a pair of black jeans and a gray T-shirt that hugs the contours of his chest.

I chose something a bit more traditional—black trousers and a suit coat, along with a white button-down shirt. Even though my days as a police detective are behind me, I feel better when I dress the part.

Ian watches me strap on my Rolex—a gift from him. "My handsome man," he says as he steps forward and straightens my collar. He pats my chest, smoothing my shirt. "Perfect."

The way he's looking at me makes my heart beat faster. I reach out to cup his face and draw him closer. As we stand nose to nose, I gaze into his eyes, bright green irises flecked with gold. "How did I get so lucky?"

He smiles. "I would argue that I'm the one who's lucky."

Immediately, my thoughts return to the circumstances of how we met, and the serious danger Ian was in after his good friend Eric Townsend was brutally murdered. And thinking about that murder case reminds me of what my life was like before I met Ian.

Those aren't happy memories. All I did was work, eat, sleep, and repeat. Day in and day out. I tried dating, but I could never connect with any of the women I went out with. There was nothing there for me—no passion, no desire. Nothing. I always had to fake it. And then, by chance, I met Ian, and my whole world turned upside down. He made me come alive, not just my body, but my heart as well.

It was a crazy fluke that Ian and I crossed paths the

night we met, not just once, but twice. If I hadn't met him when I did, I'd still be living alone in my Lincoln Park condo.

"Hey." Ian frowns as he brushes his thumb gently across my cheek, tracing the top edge of my beard. Then he runs his fingers through my short dark hair. "What's wrong?"

I mentally shake myself. There's no use dwelling on my gloomy past. "Nothing's wrong. Ready to go?" I check my watch. "We should leave."

Ian studies me a moment, as if he's hoping I'll say more. "Ready as I'll ever be," he finally says. He slips his phone into his back pocket. "You're sure you're okay?"

"I'm fine."

He doesn't look convinced. "Tonight, I'll wipe that scowl off your handsome face."

"I'm not scowling."

He laughs. "Yes, you are. But don't worry. I'll give you something else to think about later."

Smiling in spite of myself, I follow Ian out of our bedroom and down the stairs to the front door. We make a pit stop at the front coat closet so I can grab my waist holster and handgun. I have a concealed carry license and always carry a handgun whenever we're out in public. I guess it's a habit leftover from my days as a cop. Always prepared, that's my motto.

Ian slips on a jacket to ward off the cool autumn temperatures. We head out the front door and down the steps to the driveway. I grab my keys from my pocket and open the front passenger door. For routine trips, we usually take my black BMW, and I do the driving. When Ian's in the mood to show off, we take his bright blue Porsche 911.

While Ian slides into his seat, I walk around to the driver's side.

"This is exciting," Ian says as I back out of our drive and head for Superior. Gina's café is only ten minutes away.

"What is?" I ask.

"This is our first criminal case."

"It might be." Our first two cases dealt with pretty straightforward domestic issues—a wife who was having an affair with her personal trainer, and a husband with a secret gambling problem.

Ian turns to face me. "So, do you think it is one of her employees?"

"We'll see. Never jump to conclusions until you have all the facts. Basic sleuthing one-oh-one."

Ian doesn't seem deterred from his line of reasoning. "Maybe it's a mafia thing. You never know."

Ian straightens in his seat and lays his palm on my thigh. The warm weight of his hand on my leg feels good. It's little things like this that remind me of how much Ian has changed my life. Even small, mundane things become more enjoyable with him around.

"Let's not get ahead of ourselves," I say. "It's most likely one of her employees because it has to be someone with access to the building."

I stroke my thumb over the back of Ian's hand, brushing the crisp brown hairs. Even such an innocent touch like this makes my body stir.

He turns his hand over so that his palm is pressed to mine, and he links our fingers.

Ian's phone rings, and he releases my hand so he can check the screen. "Huh. That's weird. It says *caller ID unknown*." He takes the call anyway. "Hello, this is Ian." He stares out the windshield, saying nothing.

"Who is it?" I ask.

He shrugs. "Hello?" Then he ends the call. "It must have been a wrong number. I could hear someone breathing, though."

"I'm sure it was just a wrong number."

౬Ͻ **3**

Ian Alexander

Tyler parks in one of the few available parking spots in the lot behind Gina's café. His late-model black BMW suits him—it's reliable, but a bit too staid and often cranky. I have to admit, though, watching him drive is a turn-on. Tyler does everything well, including navigating the congested streets of Chicago with just one hand on the steering wheel, because he's holding mine with the other. Even during rush hour. Honestly, I don't think there's anything he can't do.

I've seen Tyler on the mat with Liam before. He can damn well hold his own. If we get in a scrape, I have zero doubt my man will save our asses. I've also seen him handle his gun—clean it, inspect it, and even shoot it. Am I weird for getting turned on while watching my boyfriend handle his weapon? His *firearm*, I mean. I'm talking about his *gun*. But he's just as competent in how he handles his body, too. And I definitely know all about *that* from firsthand experience.

Tyler kills the engine and turns in his seat to face me. "Okay, here's the plan," he says, suddenly all business. "We go in, meet with the client, and ask her some basic questions. We're information gathering at this stage. Our main goal is to find out who has access to her shop—namely, who has a key—as well as who might have a motive for stealing. Opportunity and motive are at the heart of every crime."

"Got it." I love seeing him so focused on a case. And I love how he takes the time to explain his thought processes to me.

"Gina Capelli is independently wealthy," he continues, "so this isn't about money. No, this is about the fact that someone is violating her trust. Otherwise, she'd just call the cops and let them handle it. But she hasn't done that, which tells me she's afraid it's an inside job."

I frown, imagining how betrayed I'd feel if we discovered Jerry or Kimi stealing from us. "That would suck."

"Exactly." Tyler removes his gun from the storage compartment in his center console and performs a quick check of the magazine before he slams it back in. He tucks his gun into the holster.

Okay, yeah, that was hot. Just like in the movies.

Handling a gun is second nature to him. I've never even touched one before—well, other than handling his on occasion. It's always unloaded, though, when I do.

Tyler nods toward the building's rear entrance. "Ready?"

Stoked, I reach for my door handle. "Let's do this."

Tyler smiles as he exits the vehicle to join me.

"What?" I ask.

He shakes his head. "Nothing."

"You smiled about something."

"It's just that you're—" He lays his hand on my back. "I don't think I've ever had so much fun at work before, that's all."

We walk in through the rear entrance, stepping into a hallway that leads to the café at the front of the store. We pass two gender-neutral bathrooms and a door marked PRIVATE, which I presume is Gina's office. We continue down the hallway until we reach the dining area. Even though it's after the lunch rush, the place is still packed. There's not an available table in the café. In fact, there's a line out the front door that looks like it stretches down the block.

"Popular place," I murmur as I follow Tyler up to the order counter.

My senses are completely enveloped by the aroma of deliciously flavored coffees and fresh-baked pastries and breads. I know how good their pastries are because I've had them at special events at Beth and Shane's place. Gina does all their catering—birthday parties, baby showers, even weddings.

Tyler cuts to the front of the queue. "Tyler Jamison," he says to the young man behind the counter. "We're here to see Ms. Capelli."

A young guy with a dark goatee points in the direction we just came. "Down the hallway. The manager's office is on your left. She's expecting you."

We retrace our steps until we come to the door marked PRIVATE. Tyler knocks, and a female voice says, "Come in."

Inside, we find a pretty brunette in her early thirties seated behind an old-fashioned oak desk. Her dark hair is cut chin-length, parted on the side. She's dressed in a pair of gray linen slacks and a dark blue blouse.

She waves us in. "Come on in, guys. Thanks for coming on such short notice. Have a seat." She motions to the two chairs in front of her desk.

Tyler shakes Gina's hand, and then he turns to me. "Gina, this is my partner, Ian Alexander."

At the double entendre, Tyler's lips curve up at the corners.

"Pleased to meet you, Gina," I say, biting back a grin of my own as she shakes my hand. *Yeah, we're partners in more ways than one.*

Suddenly, I realize I don't know if Gina knows Tyler's gay. He only recently came out to his family. His former boss and a few co-workers know, and our close friends do, but I don't think it's public knowledge.

"It's a pleasure to meet you, Ian." Gina says. Then she winks at me. "It's obvious what Tyler sees in you."

Well, I guess that answers that.

"I appreciate you taking my case," she says, suddenly switching to business mode. "The thefts have been going on for a couple of months, and I finally decided I'd better do something about it."

"How much money is missing?" Tyler asks.

Her shoulders fall. "At this point, about two grand."

Tyler relaxes back in his chair. "Tell us what you know."

"At least once a week, when I arrive in the morning, I find some of the proceeds from the night before missing. Usually it's around one to two hundred dollars at a time. Whoever's doing this isn't taking it all. I'm guessing they hope no one will notice."

"Why haven't you called the police?" Tyler asks.

She frowns. "I can't believe any of my employees would steal from me. We're like a family. But in the event it is one of my employees, then I'm hoping we can handle it quietly in-house. I don't want the police involved. I'm trying to keep this low-key. And I don't want my employees to think I don't trust them."

Tyler retrieves a small notepad and pen from his inside jacket pocket. "How many employees do you have?"

"Twelve. Two openers, two closers, and the rest rotate throughout the day and evenings, filling in where needed."

Tyler starts jotting down notes. "Did you do background checks before hiring them?"

"Yes. Nothing terrible jumped out at me."

"We'll need their names, contact information, and social security numbers. We'll run fresh background checks."

She winces. "I should warn you, a lot of them have rough backgrounds. It's why I hired them in the first place—to give them a fresh start. Most of them have prior convictions, and a few of them have even been incarcerated. Some are recovering addicts. But they're all clean now, and I trust them."

"Where do you keep the money at night?" Tyler asks.

She opens a side desk drawer. "In these pouches." She lifts a brown leather zippered pouch and lays it on the desk. "At night, whoever's closing counts the proceeds in the registers. We leave a few hundred in the cash drawers for the next day and place the rest in this pouch. I'm usually the one who delivers the cash to the bank the next morning, just after we open."

"When do you come in to work?"

"Around five-thirty. I'm an early bird, so I'm always one of the first ones here. Rosemary is the other opener. She comes in about the same time I do." Gina lays her hand on the leather pouch. "I count the money each morning and compare it to the receipts from the night before, so

I'm the only one who knows when some is missing."

"Who usually closes?"

"Eddy and Steve. But, Tyler," —she shakes her head adamantly— "neither of those guys would steal from me. Eddy is newly married and has a baby on the way. He'd lose everything if he got caught stealing. And Steve— well, he's as honest as the day is long. I'd trust him with my life."

"Most likely, it's the last person in the store who's stealing," Tyler says. "Or it's the first person who arrives in the morning. Who arrives first? You or Rosemary?"

"It varies, depending on which one of us gets here first. But I promise you, it's not Rosemary. There have been plenty of times when I arrived before she did and found money missing."

Tyler sighs. "Who else has access to the building? A night janitor, perhaps? Delivery people?"

Gina shakes her head. "No one. We do our own cleaning. No one else comes into the shop. That's why I don't understand how this is happening."

"Have you seen any signs of a break-in?"

"No. None."

Tyler frowns. "Gina, you need to prepare yourself for any and all possibilities. I'm sorry, but it's likely that one of your employees is stealing from you." He glances around the room. "Do you have security cameras installed on site?"

She nods. "There are cameras in the front of the store, but not back here."

"Why not?" Tyler asks.

"If I installed cameras here in my office, I'm afraid my employees would think I don't trust them. I don't want to ruin the comradery we've built."

Tyler looks around the office. "What about a safe?"

Gina points to the wall behind her. "There's an old one, but the lock is broken. We use it to hold our purses." She laughs. "It's pretty useless."

"You could get it repaired," Tyler suggests gently.

"Yeah, but then we're back to the trust issue."

Tyler sighs, but he doesn't try to convince her otherwise. "All right. Ian and I will do surveillance, starting tonight. Can you get us a key to the back door? Whoever's getting in is coming through that door. He, or she, must know there aren't any surveillance cameras back here."

Gina removes a key chain from the top desk drawer and hands it to Tyler.

"When does everyone clear out at night?" he asks.

"We officially close at nine, and clean-up takes about

an hour, so Eddy and Steve are usually out by ten."

"All right, then." Tyler looks at me. "We'll start tonight."

Before we leave, Gina hands over a print-out of her employees' contact information. "I can't imagine it's any one of them. I just can't."

* * *

"Are we seriously staking out Gina's café tonight?" I ask Tyler as we exit the building.

"Yep." He unlocks the front passenger door for me—using a *key*—very old school. He holds my door while I slide into my seat.

Such a gentleman.

His car lacks modern conveniences, such as Bluetooth and a rear camera. My Porsche, however, has all the technology bells and whistles available in the market. Still, I like riding in Tyler's car. I like watching his long fingers grip the black leather steering wheel. He handles the car like he handles me—masterfully and with confidence.

"I honestly hope it's not one of Gina's employees," I say, redirecting my thoughts back to our case. "She has so much faith in them. She'll be devastated if the thief turns out to be one of them."

"Odds are, that's exactly who it is. It has to be some-one with access to the building after hours." Tyler tucks the list Gina gave him into his jacket pocket. "We'll ask Jerry to run background checks on her employees."

My god, this is for real. We're doing background checks.

I'm super excited about the idea of doing a stakeout with Tyler tonight—just the two of us holed up in his car for *hours*, just waiting for a criminal to appear. My mind starts reeling with all the preparations we need to make. "We'll need to bring a coffee thermos and cups. And some snacks. Do you think we'll need binoculars?"

Tyler laughs. "No, we won't need binoculars. Coffee and snacks aren't a bad idea, though. We'll be sitting out-side the café all night long."

I rest my hand on Tyler's rock-hard thigh. "This is going to be fun."

He chuckles. "I'm glad you think so."

He lays his hand on top of mine, just like I hoped he would. When he rubs his palm firmly against the back of my hand, heat courses through me. We're going to be cooped up alone for hours in his car tonight. I squeeze his thigh. Who knows what could happen?

4

Tyler Jamison

Once we're back home, Ian hands the info on Gina's employees over to Jerry so he can run background checks.

"Do you know how to run background checks?" I ask him.

Jerry nods. "Piece of cake, boss."

"It's Tyler," I remind him. "There's no need to call me *boss*."

"Right, boss," he says with a sly glint in his eye.

We leave Jerry and Kimi in the carriage house and head across the driveway to the townhouse. I've noticed that Ian has slowed down a bit since his self-defense class this morning. I know how bruising those classes can be. "How are you holding up?" I ask him when we walk in through the back door.

"I'm fine. Why?"

"You're not sore?"

He gives me a sheepish look. "Hell, yes, I'm sore. My ass, my thighs, my shoulders. It gets easier, right? Please tell me it does."

"Give it time. Why don't you rest up this afternoon? We've got a long night ahead of us sitting in a car. Go upstairs and soak in the Jacuzzi. Then take a nap. I'll make dinner tonight."

He looks wary. "You don't have to. I can make dinner."

"Hey, I'll throw some potatoes in the oven and some steaks on the grill. That's easy enough even for me."

Ian looks tempted. "Are you sure you don't mind?"

"Of course, I don't. Come on, I'll walk you upstairs." I follow Ian up to our bedroom, which is located at the front of the house overlooking our quiet, tree-lined street.

He heads to the bathroom, strips down to his underwear, then comes out and throws himself down on our king-size bed. He groans. "Everything hurts."

"Poor baby," I say as I sit beside him.

"I have muscles hurting that I didn't even know I had."

I run my fingers through his hair, gently tugging the strands. When I scrape his scalp with my nails, he groans again, but this time for a different reason.

"Move over," I say, nudging him.

He rolls to the center of the mattress, onto his belly. "There was talk of a massage earlier."

I lean down beside him and whisper in his ear. "You did good today, baby. I'm proud of you."

He shivers. "You really think so?"

"Absolutely." Sitting beside him, I start by massaging his scalp. "You gave it your all. Besides, Liam McIntyre is a beast on the mat. He doesn't take it easy on anyone."

He laughs. "Except for me, maybe."

I slide my hands down to knead his neck muscles, then lower to his stiff shoulders. Based on the sounds he's making, I think Ian's enjoying the attention. He's very tactile. He loves to be touched.

"I hope you're feeling up to going to the shooting range tomorrow," I say as I continue with a gentle massage, moving down the length of one arm, then the other. "But if you're too sore, we can reschedule."

"No," he moans sleepily. "I don't want to reschedule. I can do it."

"Rome wasn't built in a day, you know. I don't expect you to be Superman."

He yawns. "I'll settle for being Robin to your Batman."

I know how much it means to him that we're working together. Investigation is nothing new to me, but he's never done anything like this before. Hell, he's never even held a job before. Fortunately, thanks to his inheritance, he's never needed to. And it's a good thing because he can't tolerate the idea of a nine-to-five office job. Sitting still in one place for long periods of time doesn't work for him.

I admit I love the idea of us working together. But after what he went through recently with Roy Valdez and then with Brad Turner, the idea of anyone hurting Ian makes me go a little crazy. I still have nightmares about seeing Roy standing on the deck of Ian's boat, gun in hand. Roy could have killed Ian if Ian's bodyguard, Miguel Rodriguez, and I hadn't been there to stop him.

After massaging Ian's arms, I start working his hands, stroking his fingers and kneading his palms.

He groans. "Oh, god, Tyler, that feels good. I'll gladly

take self-defense classes every single day of my life if this is what it gets me."

I smile as I move to his back and work my thumbs slowly along the entire length of his spine. "How does that feel?"

I'm not surprised when I don't get an answer. He had quite a workout today.

I peer down into his sleeping face. Unable to resist, I lie down beside him and stroke his hair, letting the strands curl around my fingers.

I'm always amazed that Ian could be interested in a jaded man like me. We're nothing alike. He's young and exuberant, outgoing, and an extrovert. I'm the quite opposite. It scares me sometimes when I think about how much he means to me. If he woke up one day and wondered why he was wasting his time with me, I'd be devastated. Now that I live with this ray of sunshine in my life, I couldn't bear to go back to living in the dark.

I rest my head close to his, our foreheads touching, and close my eyes. I'll rest here a bit before starting dinner. Nothing's more important at this moment than simply being near him.

I'm a little old to be acting like a love-struck fool, but I figure it's better late than never.

* * *

"I'm sorry I fell asleep on you," Ian says as he steps into our rooftop greenhouse. "God, that smells good. How's it coming?"

I flip the steaks one last time. "Just in time, sleepyhead. The potatoes should be ready, and these steaks will be done soon. I was just about to come wake you."

As Ian yawns, he stretches his back and shoulders. His T-shirt rides up, giving me a glimpse of his V-cut abs. "I didn't realize how tired I was."

He walks over to the glass wall that faces Lake Michigan in the not-too-far distance. Our townhouse is just a couple of blocks from Lake Shore Drive, which runs along the lake. We're well into autumn, and the sun sets earlier and earlier each day, casting a warm glow on the greenhouse roof.

Ian looks in the direction of the yacht club where his forty-foot baby, *Carpe Diem*, is moored. "We should take the boat out while the weather is still halfway decent. We could even cruise up the shore to your sister's place in Kenilworth."

"Sounds good. You promised to teach me how to operate it."

Ian joins me at the grill, slips his arm around my waist, and leans in close. As I catch his natural scent and a whiff of his cologne, my body tightens. When he tucks his fingers into the waistband of my jeans, a shiver races along my spine.

I lean in to kiss him and murmur, "Dinner's ready."

We load the steaks onto a platter and carry them downstairs to the kitchen. While Ian sets the table, I take the potatoes out of the oven and drop one on each of our plates, along with the butter dish and the sour cream. "I even made a salad," I say. "It's in the fridge."

Ian opens the refrigerator door and peers inside. "I'm impressed, babe."

I shrug. "It's nothing fancy. I just wanted everything to be ready when you woke up."

We gather the last couple of ingredients—a bottle of steak sauce and a raspberry vinaigrette for the salad. I grab us a couple of beers, and we sit at the kitchen table to eat.

Ian raises his bottle to me. "Thank you for a lovely dinner."

I touch the neck of my bottle to his. "My pleasure." I take a sip. "We have time for dinner and then a movie, if you want, before we have to leave for Gina's."

Ian smiles. "Dinner, a movie, *and* a stakeout. You're spoiling me."

"Don't get too excited. Stakeouts are often long and boring, not to mention physically painful. It's uncomfortable sitting cramped in a car for hours on end. And usually, it's all for naught because nothing much happens."

Ian takes a swig of his beer. "Or, we might get lucky and catch a thief."

* * *

We arrive at Gina's building at half past nine and park in the rear parking lot, as far back from the entrance as we can get while still having a clear line of sight to the door. The two employees who close up shop should be leaving soon. Their cars are parked back here.

"Coffee?" Ian asks. He brought a thermos with us, along with a bag of white cheddar popcorn and a tin of homemade chocolate chip cookies he whipped up after dinner. "Salty, sweet, and caffeine—the necessary food groups," he says.

I laugh as I reach for a cookie. "I've never been on such a well-stocked stakeout."

Looking satisfied, Ian leans his seat back a bit to get

comfortable. "I figure we should enjoy ourselves. This reminds me of going to a drive-in movie with my parents. They took me and Layla when we were little kids. We sat in the back seat with our pillows and blankets, and we always ended up falling asleep before the movie ended. It was fun, though. Our parents would sneak a kiss when they thought we weren't paying attention."

A few minutes before ten, the café lights go out.

"Heads up," I say. "They're coming out."

Sure enough, two males exit the rear door, one a tall, slender African-American man in his late twenties, the other a Caucasian man in his thirties. It's warm enough out that neither one is wearing a jacket.

Ian raises his seat into an upright position and peers out the front windshield to study the two men. "Neither one of them looks like he has anywhere to hide a few hundred bucks."

"You're right."

"So, now what?"

"Now we wait to see if anyone uninvited shows up during the night."

"How long do we wait?"

"Until either Gina or Rosemary shows up in the morning."

Ian groans. "That's like five-thirty."

I laugh "Get comfortable, Ian. We're going to be here a while."

Taking me at my word, Ian settles back in his seat and opens the bag of popcorn. He tosses a handful into his mouth, then offers me the bag. "Want some? It's really good stuff."

"Thanks." I take a handful and try not to snicker.

"What's so funny?"

"You are." And then I lean across the center console and kiss him, tasting salt and cheddar flavoring on his lips. "I don't think I've ever enjoyed a stakeout this much."

"Of course not." He laughs. "You never went on one with me before."

Midnight comes and goes. Then another couple hours crawl by. We haven't seen a soul.

Ian fidgets in his seat. "Can I get out of the car and stretch my legs? My ass is going numb."

"Sorry, no."

"Can I climb into the back seat and stretch out?"

I chuckle, thinking how much he sounds like a bored kid. "If you must. Just do it quietly."

He frowns. "Never mind."

"Ian—"

"No, I'm fine." He grabs another cookie. "I think we should buy something bigger, like an SUV. A really big one with heated seats and lots of legroom." He tries to stretch out, but there's not quite enough room.

I reach over and rub his thigh. "Restless legs?"

"Yeah."

I should have realized this would happen. Ian gets antsy when he's in a confined space for too long. Of course he does. His birth mother used to lock him in an upstairs windowless room while she got wasted and entertained tricks downstairs. I catch his hand and bring it to my mouth to kiss.

"Is it considered inappropriate to make out on a stakeout?" he asks, sounding hopeful.

I laugh. "Yes. Highly."

"Damn. Have you ever done it before?"

"Made out on a stakeout?" I give him an incredulous look. "No."

"Well, there's a first time for everything." He slides his hand between my legs and strokes the inside of my thigh while the back of his pinky finger brushes against my zipper.

I grab his hand. "You're killin' me, baby."

"Doesn't hurt to try." He looks far from innocent. "There's a first time for everything."

Around four, Ian falls asleep with his hand in mine. He's tired, so I let him rest while I keep watch. There's still no sign of anyone lurking around the café.

While I watch the back entrance, which is lit by an overhead lamp, my mind wanders. It's grown chilly this late at night. I should have thought to bring a blanket for Ian. Fortunately, I keep a jacket in the back seat. I grab it and lay it across Ian's torso.

When my eyelids start to grow heavy, I pour myself another cup of coffee. Fortunately, it's still hot. I relish the rush of caffeine as it hits my bloodstream.

At five, I'm suddenly on alert when I see headlights flash across the parking lot. It turns out to be the trash truck making its early morning rounds, emptying the dumpsters located behind Gina's building. *Nothing to see here, folks.*

Right on schedule, Gina arrives in her silver Audi at five-thirty and parks near the employee entrance. She gets out of her car, unlocks the rear door, and disappears inside the building. A moment later, the interior lights switch on. A few minutes later, Rosemary arrives.

It was a very uneventful night. My back is stiff, and my

legs ache to stretch out. I'm sure Ian's do, too.

When I start the engine, Ian wakes and raises his seat to an upright position. "What'd I miss?"

"Absolutely nothing. We can go now. Gina's at work, and there was no sign of her thief. Let's go home and get some sleep before our appointment at the shooting range."

Ian yawns as he buckles his seat belt. "Sounds good to me. Take me home, babe." Then he notices the jacket I laid over him. "Where did this come from?"

I nod toward the backseat. "I forgot I had it."

"Aw, thank you." He reaches over and pats my thigh. "You take such good care of me."

⌄ 5

Ian Alexander

I t's surreal driving through the streets of Chicago just before dawn, when the sun is starting to rise and the streetlights are still on. It's been a while since I stayed out this late. I'm so tired I can barely keep my eyes open.

When we arrive home, we park in the driveway and walk up the steps to the front door. Tyler unlocks the door, and I stumble in like a drunken sailor.

"Go up to bed," he says. "I'll lock up and join you in a minute. I need to write up some quick case notes. Just give me five minutes."

Exhausted, I do as Tyler says, making a pit stop in our bathroom to pee and brush my teeth. I strip naked, toss my clothes in the hamper, and fall into bed.

I try to wait up for Tyler, but it's a losing battle. My eyelids feel like they're weighted with lead. I'm more than half asleep when the mattress dips as Tyler climbs into bed and snuggles close. He smells good, like man, soap, and mint toothpaste. "Mm," I murmur, too tired to speak actual words.

His lips linger for a long moment against my forehead. Then he tucks me against him and wraps his arm around me, pulling me close to his bare chest. He fits his hips against my ass and tucks his knees behind mine.

"Go to sleep, baby." His voice rough and low, and he sounds as exhausted as I feel.

When I feel his lips at the back of my neck, I shiver. "G'night. Love you."

"Love you, too."

* * *

Thanks to the light-blocking curtains Tyler talked me into, our bedroom is still dark when I wake, even though it has to be late morning. I feel pretty rested, so I know we got some decent sleep after we arrived home at dawn. I check the time on my phone. It's one o'clock in the afternoon. We got a little over six hours of sleep.

Right now, I have the bed all to myself, so I indulge in a full-body stretch, groaning loudly.

Tyler strolls into our bedroom, dressed in faded blue jeans and a navy-blue T-shirt that lovingly hugs his torso. My belly does a somersault at the sight of him looking all sexy and disheveled. He still has bed head.

I rejoice when he offers me a cup of coffee that smells like caramel and vanilla. "Gimme!" I say, reaching out. "You really do love me, don't you?"

"Perfect timing. I was just coming up to wake you. We have to leave soon for the shooting range. How do you feel?"

I take a sip of my deliciously sweet coffee and sigh. "Mm, thank you. This is just what I needed. And I feel wonderful."

"You're not sore from yesterday?"

"From what? The self-defense class or the stakeout?"

He chuckles. "Both."

"Nah, I feel great." I set my cup down on the bedside table and stand. We're both barefoot, so we're eye to eye, but he's fully dressed, while I'm butt naked. I also woke with an erection that won't quit."

Tyler glances down at my morning wood.

"You should have awakened me when you got up," I say, noticing where he's looking.

I groan when Tyler wraps his long fingers around me and squeezes firmly. He leans in and kisses me. "I thought about it, but I figured you needed the sleep."

"More than I need you?" I thrust into his fist and moan as he strokes me. "Never."

Smiling, Tyler shoves me gently back onto the bed. "We have just enough time."

"For what?" But I know exactly what he's talking about. I just want to hear him say it.

"For me to make you feel good." He kneels between my thighs and takes me in his mouth. And then I can't even think straight.

* * *

"Are you nervous?" Tyler asks as we pull into the shooting range parking lot.

We park in a visitor slot in front of a large concrete and steel building. It's the most unattractive building

I've ever seen, with absolutely no character at all. We're in an industrial area, and the property is surrounded by a tall metal chain-link fence and lots of video cameras.

"No, I'm not nervous." *Hell, yes, I'm nervous. I've never shot a gun before. For fuck's sake. What if I accidentally shoot Tyler?*

Tyler chuckles. "Don't worry. You'll do fine."

I turn to face him. "Yeah? What if I shoot you? Huh? What then?"

He struggles to keep a straight face. "That's not going to happen."

"How do you know?"

"Because the first thing we'll do is go over safety."

I feel somewhat relieved. "Am I going to shoot your gun?"

Tyler shakes his head. "I think we'll start you on something a little easier. My Glock has quite a kick."

"But *you're* giving me the lesson, right? Not someone else?"

"Right. I'm doing it." He reaches over and squeezes my thigh. "Relax. There's nothing to worry about."

I unbuckle my seatbelt and lean close to him so I can press my lips to his. "Please don't laugh if I suck at this."

His hand slides behind my neck, and he squeezes gently. "I'd never laugh at you."

"Yeah, well don't expect too much. We can't all be Superman."

Tyler rolls his eyes at me. "I thought I was Batman. Make up your mind."

Huffing, I open my door, step out of the car, and follow him into the building.

We stop at the front registration desk, where a middle-aged, African-American woman greets Tyler by name. Obviously, they know him around here.

According to her name tag, she's Rochelle. "Good afternoon, Detective. Cooper's expecting you." Then she gives me a knowing smile. "And you must be *Ian*."

I nod. Apparently, they know about me, too.

Rochelle hands us each a guest badge to clip to our shirts. Then she buzzes us through a locked metal door.

On the other side of the door is a completely different world. The space is cavernous and filled with people. There's a counter to our left, behind which is a wall displaying every kind of rifle imaginable. A glass counter displays countless handguns. There are two guys behind the counter helping the people waiting in line. Straight ahead is a glass partition, and beyond the glass are lanes for target practice. Each lane is separated by a wall, and at the end of each lane a paper target hangs from a wire.

"Let's get you a good beginner gun to practice with," Tyler says as he leads me to a display counter. In the glass cabinet below are three rows of black handguns, all shapes and sizes.

"Hey, guys," Cooper says as he steps up to the counter. "What can I get you?"

Tyler points through the glass at a neat little black handgun on the top shelf. "Let's start him off with this Smith and Wesson M&P EZ Shield."

Cooper nods as he retrieves the gun in question and lays it on the counter. "Good choice." He selects a box of ammo from the shelves behind him and hands it to Tyler. "Grab yourselves some targets, then pick up your ear and eye protection before you head into the shooting range."

Cooper sets the gun and the box of ammo in a plastic caddy. Then he points to a rack of large, colorful sheets of paper. "Grab some targets and have at it."

"Take a few," Tyler says as we pass the rack of paper. "It doesn't matter which ones."

I select a few sheets that have outlines of the human body on them, with concentric circles over the head and chest.

When we reach the entrance to the shooting range, a woman on duty hands us each a heavy pair of black earmuffs.

"Ear protection," Tyler says as he slips his on. "It's loud in there."

The woman hands each of us a pair of clear goggles. "Eye protection."

I'm surprised by how well the earmuffs mute the sound around us. I follow Tyler through another heavy metal door. Once we're inside the shooting range, I flinch every time I hear the boom of a shot fired. Even with the earmuffs, I can still hear what sounds like explosions.

"You'll get used to the noise," Tyler says. His voice is muffled by my earmuffs, but I can still hear him.

Tyler walks down the row of shooting lanes until he comes to an empty stall. I follow him in and watch as he sets the gun and box of ammo on a counter.

"You shoot a Glock, right?" I ask.

Tyler nods.

"Yours looks bigger. Your gun."

He grins. "Really? We're going to debate whose is bigger?"

I jab him with my elbow. "You know what I mean. So, you're starting me off with a baby gun?"

Tyler laughs. "Ian, there's no such thing as a baby gun. All handguns are capable of doing serious damage to the human body. But the recoil of this M&P EZ Shield isn't quite as strong as my Glock's, so it's a good gun for you to start off with. You can try my Glock, too, and see which one you prefer."

He pops the little cartridge thing out of the gun's handle and holds it up to me. "This is called a *magazine*. It's empty at the moment, see?"

I nod.

Then he slides the top of the gun back showing me an empty cavity. "This is the chamber. It's currently empty, too."

Again, I nod.

Tyler slams the empty magazine back into the gun handle, then holds it out to me. "It's not loaded; we just confirmed that. First, I want you to get a feel for the gun in your hand."

Tyler holds the gun out to me, and as I reach for it, he pulls it back. "Rule number one, never point a gun at another person unless you intend to shoot them. Got it?"

I nod. "Sure. But it's not even loaded."

"Doesn't matter. Always assume a gun is loaded."

He hands me the gun, and I point it safely at the floor.

"Also, don't point it at your foot," he says. "I can't tell you how many people have shot themselves in the foot—literally." He lifts my hand in the air. "Wrap your fingers around the grip, like this. How does that feel?"

"Cold. And it's much heavier than I expected."

Tyler moves my index finger away from the trigger area. "Rule number two. Keep your finger away from the trigger until you're ready to shoot. Make it a habit. These triggers are very sensitive. It doesn't take much pressure to fire a gun. Got it?"

I nod. "Got it."

Tyler loads one of the paper targets onto the wire and sends it out about a dozen yards in front of us. Then he turns me so that I'm facing the target. "Let me show you how to hold it and how to aim." He steps in close and wraps his arms around me to demonstrate how I should hold the gun. His arms close in on my sides.

His breath ruffles the hair at the back of my head as he speaks. "See the white dot at the tip of the muzzle? Using your dominant eye, line the dot up with your target. Hold your breath, remain steady, then squeeze the trigger." He pulls the trigger to demonstrate. Of course nothing happens as it's not loaded. "Now you try."

I do my best to copy what Tyler did, and I pull the

trigger.

"Now, let me teach you how to load it." He takes the gun back from me, careful to point the muzzle down and away. "Pop out the magazine and start loading the rounds."

He demonstrates popping one bullet into the magazine after another, until it's half-full. Then he hands it to me. "You do the rest."

I repeat his action until the magazine is full. "Now what?"

Tyler shows me how to slam the magazine into the gun's handle. He also explains how the safety switch works. "All right, go ahead. Take your time. There's no rush."

I do as he says, holding the gun securely in both hands and lining up the target, and then I pull the trigger. When the gun jumps wildly in my hands, accompanied by a loud crack, I flinch. "Holy shit, that's loud!" I study the paper target and realize I missed it completely. "Crap. I missed."

Tyler laughs. "It's okay. Try again. Line up your sight with the target. Tighten your grip, hold your breath, keep your aim steady, and then squeeze the trigger."

Tyler stands behind me, his hands on my waist,

steadying me. I close one eye, focus on the dot—which is pointed at the center of the target—then squeeze the trigger.

Crack!

This time there's a hole in the paper, on the far right edge, about a foot from the spot I was aiming for. "Wow. I hit it. Sort of."

Tyler laughs. "Hey, you hit the target on your second try. That's pretty good."

"Really?"

He nods. "Really. Now try again."

I'm pretty sure he's humoring me, but I appreciate the moral support anyway.

6

Tyler Jamison

While Ian's in the shower, I get a text message from a local jewelry company telling me that our wedding bands are ready to be picked up. I head downstairs, so Ian won't overhear me, and call Layla.

"Hey, Tyler," she says with a laugh.

She definitely sounds like she's in a good mood. I can hear Jason's voice in the background. They've been splitting their time between Jason's apartment, which is just a few blocks away from us, and Layla's parents' house. It's a good transition strategy for her. Too much change at once could have a negative impact on her mental health. But I know Jason won't let that happen. He's not just her boyfriend; he's her medically-trained bodyguard.

"Hey, Layla. How's it going?"

"Great. What's up?"

"I'm calling to ask a favor."

"Sure. Anything," she says.

"I just found out our wedding bands are ready to be picked up. I'd like to pick them up this afternoon, without Ian knowing, so I can surprise him with them tomorrow. I was hoping you guys could stop by and distract him while I run out to pick up the rings."

"Of course we can!" She squeals so loudly I have to hold the phone away from my ear. After she fills Jason in, she returns to the line. "This is so exciting!"

I check my watch. "Do you think you could stop by soon?"

I can hear the two of them murmuring in the background. Then Layla says, "Absolutely. We're at Jason's apartment, so we're practically just around the corner. How about half an hour?"

"That's perfect, Layla. Thanks."

As I end the call, I can still hear the shower running upstairs. Ian's getting ready for our dinner plans tonight at my sister's place. But we've got a few hours until we have to leave. It's enough time for me to pick up the rings. I plan to take Ian to the St. James Yacht club tomorrow morning. We'll visit his boat, maybe even take it out on the lake if the nice weather holds. That boat is his happy place, so that's where I want to officially propose.

As I climb the stairs, the water shuts off. By the time I walk into the bathroom, Ian's standing just outside the walk-in shower, a teal-colored towel wrapped around his waist. He's using a microfiber towel to dry his hair. For a moment, I stand there watching him, enjoying the view. His body is a work of art—long limbs, lean muscles. Looking at him does things to me. He makes me feel things I'd never felt before I met him.

When he stops drying his hair, he realizes he has an audience. He motions to his half-naked body. "You want some of this?"

"You know I do." My voice sounds rough even to my own ears. "Drop the towel."

His cheeks are flushed, but I'm not sure if it's from the hot shower or from the fact that I'm openly staring at his naked body, while I'm fully dressed. I'm a bit of a controlling SOB, and that turns Ian on.

Never once taking his eyes off me, he drops the towel from around his waist and lets it fall to his feet. His nostrils flare as he sucks in a breath, his chest and shoulders rising. His belly clenches, and his dick lengthens.

I walk over and cradle his face in my hands. The longing in his expression takes my breath away. I stroke my thumbs across his cheeks. "You are so fucking beautiful."

His eyes widen. "You really think so?"

I nod, amazed by his humility. "I thought so from the very first moment I laid eyes on you."

"At the pier?"

He was the only partial witness to a murder I was investigating one night at the yacht club. I shake my head. "Before then. At Tanks, when we crossed paths in the hallway leading to the men's room. When I saw you, my heart nearly stopped."

Ian slides his hands up my sleeves to clasp my biceps. "Do you know what I wanted to do the moment I saw you?"

My dick hardens in anticipation because I'm pretty sure I can guess.

Ian drops to his knees on the plush rug beneath our feet. His hands go to my belt buckle, and he has my trousers unfastened in a heartbeat. "I wanted to do this." And then he tugs my slacks and underwear down to my ankles and takes my erection in his warm hands. He only has to squeeze me lightly, stroking just a few times, before I'm fully hard as a rock.

Gazing up at me, he licks his lips, sending fire sweeping through me. My abs tighten and my belly quivers. When he takes me into his mouth, I dig my fingers in his hair and hold on for dear life.

* * *

Just as we're getting dressed, the doorbell rings. "I'll get it," I say.

I open the front door and invite Layla and Jason in. "Perfect timing. Ian will be right down."

They step inside just as Ian reaches the foyer.

"Hey guys, hi," Ian says, a bit breathless. "What brings you here?"

Layla shrugs. "We were running errands and thought we'd stop by to say hello."

Ian pulls his sister close for a hug. "What a great surprise. Can I get you guys something to drink?"

"I'd love something cold," Layla says as her gaze bounces from Ian to me. "I'm parched."

"Sure. Come with me," he says. Always the perfect host, Ian leads the way to the kitchen.

"Ian, I need to run out for a bit," I call after him. "I've got an errand I need to take care of."

"Sure!" He's already fully distracted by our company. "Don't be long. We have dinner tonight at your sister's."

But he's already around the corner and in the kitchen. When I hear the fridge door open, that's my cue. I grab my jacket and head out the door.

I walk over to Rush Street to grab a taxi. It'll be faster this way, since I won't have to bother with parking downtown. It's just a ten-minute trip by car to the jewelry store where Ian and I purchased our wedding bands. Mine is a traditional, plain gold men's wedding band. His is also a gold band, but more slender than mine, with three small diamonds embedded in it.

The taxi drops me off right in front of the jewelry store. After paying the fare, I step out of the cab and walk inside the shop.

A pretty blonde standing behind a sales counter catches my gaze and smiles. "How can I help you?"

"I'm here to pick up two wedding bands. The name's Jamison. I received a text telling me they're ready."

She looks up our order on a computer, then nods. "I'll be right back with those." She disappears into a back room and returns a few minutes later holding a pair of velvet ring boxes, which she sets on the counter. "Here they are. Take a look."

I open the first box to find my plain gold band. Then I open the box containing Ian's ring. The diamonds are tiny, yet they sparkle with fire in the light. I pick up the ring box and tilt it this way and that, watching the light glint off the facets. "He's going to love it. Thank you."

"Would you like to try yours on?"

I set Ian's box on the counter and retrieve my band and slip it on my ring finger. It fits perfectly, and it feels good—solid and weighty. For a moment I just stare at my hand. I never dreamed I'd see a wedding band on my finger. Hell, I'm forty-five years old and this is my first real relationship.

"Do you like it?" the saleswoman asks.

I swallow past the knot in my throat. "Yes."

She smiles. "Good." Then she glances down at Ian's wedding band. "Congratulations to the both of you. I hope your fiancé likes his ring, too."

"I know he will." It occurs to me that I'm buying two men's wedding bands, and the saleswoman doesn't even bat an eye. "Thanks."

She smiles as she puts both ring boxes in a bag. Then she hands me the receipt, which I tuck into my wallet.

Outside the store, I flag down a taxi for the return trip home.

On the drive back to the townhouse, I can't stop staring at my hand. I haven't taken my ring off yet, but I'll have to before I arrive home. I just can't get over seeing a wedding band on my finger.

It's unreal. Before long, I'll be a married man.

The next step, after I officially propose and give him his ring, is for us to plan the details—the *when* and the *where* of how we'll tie the knot. Frankly, I don't care. He can have whatever he wants—a big church wedding or a quiet family ceremony. Or we could get married at the courthouse. I honestly don't care. I just want us to be officially and legally married. The details are immaterial to me.

When the taxi pulls up in front of our house, I pay the fare and climb out of the vehicle. As I walk up the steps to the front door, I remove my wedding band and slip it into my pocket.

I made good time. I was only gone an hour. When I walk through the front door, Ian and our guests are seated in the living room to my left, drinking sparkling water.

Ian jumps to his feet. "Hey, you're back." He comes to greet me, sliding his arms around my waist. He kisses the edge of my jaw. "Did you complete your errand?"

"I did." I return his hug. "So, what'd I miss?"

$\mathcal{C}$ 7

Tyler Jamison

We arrive at the penthouse that evening just before six. I park in the underground garage, and we take the private elevator up to the top floor. Shane owns the apartment building, and the entire top floor is his. He and my sister share the sprawling penthouse with Cooper and his partner, Sam.

Cooper's not just Shane's best friend—he's his right-hand man and business partner. They started McIntyre Security together after getting out of the Marines

Corp over a decade ago. While Shane is the front man—the CEO and the face of the company—Cooper seems happy to take a back seat. The former sharpshooter now runs the company's shooting range and weapons training center.

But most importantly to me, Cooper's like a father to my sister. Beth was a baby when our father died. I was eighteen at the time, so of course I remember Dad well. She has no memories of him, and that breaks my heart. She doesn't know what an amazing man he was. But Cooper fills that role for her now, and he does a damn fine job of it.

When the elevator doors open, we step out into the private foyer that leads into the penthouse. The foyer door is open, and we hear the bustling activity going on in the great room and kitchen.

It doesn't surprise me one bit to see Cooper giving my eighteen-month-old blond-haired nephew, Luke, a ride on his broad shoulders. Or to see my mom seated on one of the sofas in the living room. What's surprising is the pretty red-haired woman seated next to Mom, with my newborn niece, Ava, asleep in her arms.

"Hey, guys!" Cooper calls as he jogs over to greet us. "Welcome."

Immediately, Luke reaches for Ian. "Een!"

Cooper hands the boy over to Ian, who gives him a hug. "Hey, little guy. How's it going?"

"Een!" Then Luke looks my way and studies me rather seriously before he holds his arms out toward me.

I take him from Ian and prop the kid on my hip. He reaches up to pat my bearded cheek, and then he promptly throws himself back toward Cooper.

"Up, up," Luke says, pointing to Cooper's shoulder.

Cooper sits Luke back up onto his shoulders. "Hey, guys, come meet Rachel, Sam's sister. She's visiting from Ohio. She came to take care of the kids while Beth starts back to work."

We follow Cooper across the spacious open floor plan to a seating area where two sofas and a couple of upholstered armchairs are positioned around a stone hearth that extends up to the high, vaulted ceiling.

"Guys, this is Rachel Harrison," Cooper says. "Rachel, this is Tyler Jamison, Beth's brother, and his partner, Ian Alexander."

Rachel, who looks to be in her early thirties, smiles up at us. "It's a pleasure to finally meet you two. I've heard so much about you from these guys."

"All good, I hope," Ian says.

"Of course," she says.

"When did you get into town?" I ask her.

"Two days ago. I offered to babysit so Beth could start back to work. Ava's still so young that Beth didn't want to take her to the bookstore quite yet. And, so here I am, Aunty Rachel, babysitter extraordinaire."

"Rachel's a pediatric nurse," Cooper explains. "She took a leave of absence from the hospital where she works to come see us."

"How long will you be here?" Ian asks.

She shrugs. "I'm thinking a month, maybe longer. Who knows?" She smiles down at the sleeping baby's face. "I'm in no rush to go home." She frowns. "It was definitely time for a change of scenery."

Ava's sleeping soundly in Rachel's arms, wrapped in a soft, pale-yellow blanket. All we can see is her sweet little round face and the tuft of brown hair on her head.

My mother stands to greet us, hugging Ian first, and then me. Secretly, I'm pleased that she hugged him first. They've hit it off so well.

"How's my handsome son?" she asks me.

My mom is a beautiful woman, tall and slender, with long silvery-blonde hair. Courtesy of her Swedish roots, she has startling clear blue eyes. My sister looks so much like her, it's uncanny. Mom's in her mid-sixties. She's been a widow for over two decades, since my father, a police officer, died in the line of duty. To my knowledge, she hasn't dated since, and that's a shame.

"Did you drive?" I ask her.

"No. I took an Uber. I don't like driving downtown in the dark."

"You should have called me. We could have picked you up. We'll drive you home. Is Beth home yet?" I glance around looking for my sister who only recently started back to work after taking maternity leave.

"She should be home any minute now," Mom says. "She texted me from the car."

Almost as soon as she says that, the elevator chimes and the doors open. A moment later, Beth and Sam walk in. As soon as Luke sees his mama, he squeals and starts fighting to get down. Cooper sets him on his feet, and Luke runs to my sister.

Joe Rucker comes in right behind them. He's a tall, muscular African-American man, former Army and a former heavyweight boxer. Joe is Beth's chauffeur and another McIntyre Security employee.

"Joe, it's good to see you." We shake hands. "What brings you here?"

His gaze drifts across the room to where Mom and Rachel are seated. "I came up to see the new baby," he says in his deep bass voice. His attention lingers across the room a moment before he turns back to me. "How's the new PI venture coming along? I heard you two are working cases now."

"We are. We're both fully licensed, and Ian's taking self-defense and gun-training classes."

Joe nods toward Ian. "Good idea. It pays to be prepared for anything."

I like Joe. He's in his late fifties, very capable and reliable. From the little I know about him, he's a widower with two grown kids. And, he happens to have a thing for my mom. I have absolutely nothing against Joe, but I'm not sure how I feel about the idea of someone attempting to court my mom. She's older than he is, but he doesn't seem to mind. If she did decide to date, she couldn't pick a better man than Joe. He's a real gentleman, and I know he'd treat her like a queen.

"Mama," Luke says as he raises his arms up to Beth. "Up. Up."

She picks him up and kisses his forehead. "Hello, my sweet boy. Were you good for Aunty Rachel today?

"He was an angel," Rachel says.

Luke leans his head against Beth's shoulder and says, plaintively, "Eat."

Cooper tickles Luke's side. "You're always hungry, little man. Don't worry, dinner's ready. We're just waiting on your daddy to get home."

Mom comes forward to hug Beth. "Welcome home, dear," she says.

The last to arrive is Shane. The elevator doors open once more, and Shane walks into the penthouse.

"Dada!" Luke cries as he reaches for Shane.

"All right, everybody, let's eat!" Cooper says.

The dining room table is large enough to easily seat us all. Shane sits at one end, with Beth seated to his left. Luke's highchair is squeezed in between them.

Ian and I are seated across the table from Beth, Cooper, and Sam.

I grew up in a small family. It was just Mom and Dad and me for years, until Beth was born—their late-in-life surprise. I was already eighteen then, ready to start college. And then Dad was killed, and suddenly it was just me and Mom and a newborn baby. I'm not used to big families and crowded dining room tables. When my sister married Shane, our family grew exponentially overnight. And now with Ian in my life, it's grown again to include the Alexanders.

Sipping coffee, I sit back and take in the chatter around the table. Ian and Ingrid are discussing a new recipe for brownies. Joe, who was coaxed into staying for dinner by my matchmaking sister, hangs on Ingrid's every word.

* * *

After dinner, I manage to get my mom and sister alone for a moment in Luke's nursery. "I have something to show you." I pull Ian's ring box out of my suit coat pocket and open it. They both stare wide-eyed at the slender gold band tucked inside.

"It's beautiful," Beth whispers. "Has he seen it yet?"

"No. Not since I picked up the rings this afternoon. I'm going to surprise him with it tomorrow."

My mom runs her index finger across the three tiny diamonds embedded in the band. "He's going to love it." Then she glances up at me. "Where's yours?"

I fish around in my trouser pocket and pull out my ring, holding it out on my palm.

"Put it on," she urges.

I slip it onto my finger.

"Oh, Tyler." Mom reaches for my hand as her eyes fill

with tears.

"I've wanted this for you for so long," Beth says, fighting tears. She squeezes my hand tightly.

I have to blink several times myself to keep from tearing up, too.

8

Ian Alexander

One of the perks of being in Tyler's life is gaining a bonus family. His mom and sister have welcomed me with open arms. I didn't have to prove myself to them. I didn't have to win them over. They accepted me unconditionally. I love their son, and that's enough for them.

It's a big adjustment, being around so many people at once. When I was growing up, it was just the four of us. Tonight, there are nine of us, not including the two little kids. Beth invited Joe to stay for dinner, and he seemed more than happy to accept. I think he's got a crush on Miss Ingrid, as he calls her.

Beth and Shane take turns helping Luke with his food. Rachel's holding Ava, who's sound asleep despite all the chatter. Eventually, Ava gets passed around the table, from Rachel to Ingrid to Joe.

I get a kick out of watching the big man cradle a tiny infant in his brawny arms. "Have you got any kids, Joe?"

He nods. "Two. A son and a daughter. My daughter is married and has kids. My son is still single." He chuckles. "I've changed my share of diapers back in the day. Their poor mama died shortly after my son's birth, so I did most of the raisin' myself, with help from my own mama."

Ava is passed to me next. Feeling her slight, warm weight in my arms is almost magical. For a moment, I imagine what Tyler's baby would look like—hair as dark as midnight and eyes the color of the Caribbean, a mesmerizing blue-green eyes. Girl or boy, it wouldn't matter. He or she would be *Tyler's* baby. I realize I want that more than anything. I want Tyler's baby to care for and love. I suppose it's not out of the question. After we're married, we could find a surrogate to carry our baby.

I wonder if Sam and Cooper have given any thought to having kids one day. They'd both be great dads.

With little warning, Ava wakes up and starts fussing.

"That's my cue," Beth says with a laugh as she rises to her feet. "Somebody's hungry." She takes the baby from me and disappears down the hallway that leads to the nursery.

"Mama," Luke complains, frowning as he watches his mother disappear from sight. He leans across the high-chair tray, reaching after her retreating figure. His lips turn down in a pout. "Mama!"

Shane reaches over to ruffle his son's hair. "Mama will be right back, buddy. Here, have a bite of mashed potato."

When we're done eating, Sam and I help clear the table. Ingrid joins us in the kitchen.

When my phone buzzes in my pocket, I pull it out and glance at the screen.

Unknown number: where were u last night?

I stare at the message, trying to make sense of it.

Unknown number: u were out all night. I waited for u to come home.

These messages are creeping me out. My heart skips a beat as I text back. This has to be a mistake. *Please, let it be a mistake.*

Ian: You have the wrong number

Unknown number: No I don't

"Is everything all right?" Ingrid asks when she catches me staring at my phone.

I smile to hide my uneasiness as I slip my phone back into my pocket. "Yes, fine. It was a wrong number." But I can't shake the feeling that it wasn't. There's only one person I know who would send a message like that— Brad Turner. I thought he was out of our lives for good. Apparently, I was wrong. Just thinking about him sends a chill down my spine.

While everyone's having coffee and dessert, I go in search of Beth and find her in the nursery. She's rocking Ava, who has finished nursing. Beth's got the baby propped up on her shoulder and is trying to get her to burp.

I sit on the footstool facing the rocking chair. "She's so beautiful."

Beth smiles. "I'm a bit biased, but I think so, too." She rubs Ava's back. "She's such an easy baby."

I reach out and stroke Ava's soft brown hair. "She's got her daddy's hair."

Smiling, Beth nods. "Do you want kids?"

"Yeah. I keep imagining what Tyler's baby would look like."

"Have you guys talked about it?"

"A little. I mean, yes. He says he wants kids. We both do. But I want *Tyler's* baby, you know? I want a little baby with dark hair and blue-green eyes."

"I know exactly what you mean." She stands. "Come practice your diapering skills."

She carries Ava to the changing table, lays her down, and steps back to let me do the honors.

"I think you'd make a great dad," she says. "Nothing would make me happier than to see you and my brother parenting together."

* * *

That evening, after we return home and get ready to head out on our second night staking out Gina's café, I hop up onto the bathroom counter and watch Tyler brush his teeth. "Luke and Ava are adorable."

"Mm-hm." When he's done brushing, he rinses and wipes his mouth on a tissue. "Yes, they are."

"You'd be a fantastic father."

He smiles. "I'm not sure about that, but I know you

would. You're a natural with kids. I have no idea what I'm doing."

"You're strong and protective, and you'd keep them safe. That's what matters."

Tyler steps between my knees and leans in to kiss me. "And you'd spoil them rotten, wouldn't you?"

I grin. "Probably."

"Are you ready to go on your second stakeout?"

"Absolutely. I packed fresh coffee and snacks."

"Of course you did," he says as he follows me out of our bedroom.

It's dark outside when we leave to go to Gina's. We're not even off our street when my phone buzzes with an incoming text. Dreading what I might see, I look at the screen.

Unknown number: Where are u going this late at night?

Oh, my god, he's watching us.

My stomach drops like a stone. "Tyler."

"Yes?"

"I think someone's watching us."

"What?" Tyler shoots me an incredulous look. "What are you talking about?"

"Someone texted me earlier this evening when we were at your sister's. The caller ID said *unknown number*, so I don't know who it was. But he was asking me where I was last night. I said he had the wrong number, and he said he didn't. And now he's asking where we're going this late at night. He's got to be watching us."

Tyler's jaw clenches. "Son-of-a-bitch! It's Turner. It has to be." He automatically glances in his rearview mirror to see if we're being followed.

I look behind us, but there's no one there.

Tyler tightens his grip on the steering wheel. "Why in the hell didn't you tell me this earlier?"

"Because I knew it would upset you."

Tyler slams a fist on the steering wheel. "Damn right, I'm upset! Why didn't you tell me sooner?"

To my mortification, tears spring into my eyes. "You almost went to prison the last time you fought with Brad. Do you think I want to risk that again? I was afraid for you."

A myriad of emotions crosses his features, ranging from anger to concern to sympathy. Ultimately, it's the sympathy that wins out. "I appreciate what you're doing, Ian, but you don't need to protect me. It's supposed to be the other way around. I'm supposed to protect you."

I clutch his arm. "It goes both ways, you know. I can protect you, too."

Tyler's expression softens. "You're right. But please don't ever keep something like this from me. Turner is unhinged. There's no telling what he's capable of doing."

We arrive at Gina's building, and just like we did the night before, we park in the shadows and watch. And like last night, it's all quiet. There's not much to see. Tyler sits staring at the café's exit, lost in thought.

When I silently reach for his hand, he links our fingers and rests our hands on his thigh. Neither one of us says anything more about Brad Turner, but I know we're both thinking about it. I had hoped Brad would simply leave us alone after the court case was settled, but apparently that's not the case.

"How long has he been messaging you?" Tyler finally asks me.

"Just this evening, when we were at your sister's house. And there was an anonymous phone call yesterday, but the caller didn't say anything. That might have been him. I'm not sure."

Tyler holds out his hand. "Let me see your phone."

My heart pounds as I lay my phone in his palm.

Without a word, Tyler skims the messages from the unknown number. "God damn it."

Just before dawn comes around again, Gina and Rosemary show up at the coffee shop. It was another quiet and uneventful night.

"Is it always going to be this boring?" I ask as Tyler starts the engine.

He laughs as we drive away. "I wish."

9

Tyler Jamison

*I*t's dark when we enter Gina's café. Only a small sliver of moonlight streams through the window. I pull out my flashlight, switch it on, and light the way, while my other hand grips my Glock. "Stay behind me, Ian."

As Ian silently shadows me, we move down the hallway toward the manager's office. The office door is open just a crack, and there's a faint light visible from inside the room. We hear someone rummaging through the desk drawers. Suddenly, it's quiet, and then we hear the tell-tale sound *of a zipper. It's the money pouch. Someone's stealing cash from Gina's desk.*

I feel Ian's presence behind me, and I wish I had a free hand so I could reach back and touch him, just to reassure him. And, if I'm being honest, partly to reassure myself that he's out of harm's way. But I don't have a free hand.

A sense of dread spreads through me, and I can't shake this fear that Ian's going to get hurt. He's not ready for this. I'm afraid he'll never be ready to confront potential violence. I want to send him away. I want him to go home and wait for me there. Searching a dark building is no big deal for me. As a cop, I did it hundreds of times. But with Ian involved, everything has changed.

I turn off my flashlight and shove it into my back pocket as I approach the door, careful to keep out of sight of anyone who might be in that room. Ian stays behind me as instructed. There's a crash from within the office, followed by a muttered curse. The perpetrator must have knocked something off the desk.

Just as I'm about to kick the door open and confront the perp, I hear the sound of a slide being racked behind us. I freeze, my blood running cold when I realize there are two perps—one in the office and one behind us in the hallway. How could I have been so careless?

"If you move, I'll blow his fucking head off."

At the sound of an unfamiliar, grating voice, my heart slams into my ribcage.

Immediately, I raise my gun into the air, pointed at the ceiling. "Take it easy," I say calmly, hoping to defuse the situation.

"Hand it over," the gruff voice demands.

He snatches the gun from my hand. When he shoves Ian into me, I turn to steady him. I find myself with my back to the wall, Ian facing me. I glance down at his expression, and even in the dark, I can see fear in his eyes.

I wrap my arm around him and hold him close.

It's okay, baby.

But it's not okay. This asshole is pointing a 9mm at the back of Ian's head.

I swallow hard and try to think of a way out of this. If I was alone, I'd go for his gun. I'd risk it. But I don't dare do that with Ian standing between us. It's far too dangerous.

Damn it. It wasn't supposed to happen like this.

The door to the office opens, and the first perp walks out.

"What do we do with them?" the second guy says, the one pointing a gun at Ian.

"What d'you think?" the first guy asks. "They're witnesses. Eliminate them."

My stomach twists painfully as Ian clutches my waist. He's practically clinging to me.

This is my fault. He's in danger because I didn't have the strength to make him stay home.

"Fine," the second perp says as he presses the muzzle of his gun against Ian's scalp.

Ian looks up at me, his gaze searching mine. As he stares intently, I realize he wants my face to be the last thing he sees.

"I'm sorry," Ian whispers. "I should have listened to you."

"No, baby. I'm the one who's sorry." I tighten my hold on him.

The thundering crack of gunfire sends me shooting up out of bed. A second later I'm pacing beside the bed, frantic and disoriented. My heart is pounding, and there's a roaring in my head.

Ian sits up, the sheet falling to his waist. "What's wrong, babe?" His voice is groggy.

I'm at a loss for words, pacing as I run my fingers through my hair, pulling hard on the strands as I try to catch my breath. How can I tell him I dreamt I got him killed?

Ian crawls to my side of the bed. A moment later, he's standing in front of me, firmly gripping my arms.

"What's wrong?"

All I can do is stare at his face and remind myself he's okay. He's not dead. There's not a huge hole blown through the back of his skull. "I had a bad dream."

He grabs my hand and tugs me toward him. "It must have been a doozy. Now come back to bed."

Despite the fact my adrenaline is still through the roof, and I can't stop shaking, I let him pull me onto the mattress.

"Come here," he says as I lie back on my pillow. "It's okay. Everything's fine." He pulls me into his arms. "That must have been one helluva dream."

I laugh shakily. "That's an understatement."

"Do you want to talk about it? Sometimes it's easier when you talk about it."

"Thanks, but no." Ian's death—even in a dream—isn't something I can talk about.

Ian falls quickly back to sleep, but I lie awake for a long time. This nightmare has dredged up another nightmare—the day my dad was killed in the line of duty. He was a Chicago patrol officer, responding to a domestic violence call. Those are probably the most dangerous calls for police to respond to. On that day, when I was just eighteen years old, my father was shot dead by an enraged husband who attempted to kill his wife. My dad stepped between them as he tried to talk the husband down, and he died on the spot for his efforts.

My dad tried to be a hero, and it got him killed.

If I lose Ian, I won't survive.

*　*　*

It takes me at least an hour to fall back to sleep. When I wake again, at noon, Ian's sound asleep in my arms. He hasn't moved an inch.

As I glance down at his profile, my chest aches. The horrific nightmare is still fresh in my head.

My greatest fear is that Ian will get hurt because of me. Because he *met* me. Because our lives intertwined, and he decided he wanted to become a private investigator, like me.

I don't know what to do about it. If I tell him he can't work with me, he'll be crushed. And I'd rather cut off my own arm than hurt him. Maybe we could limit the cases we accept to those of missing pets or stolen bicycles. Maybe that would be safe enough.

Eventually, Ian stirs, moaning as he stretches. "Good morning," he murmurs.

I kiss his forehead. "Good morning."

"What time is it?"

"Noon."

He laughs. "I never thought I'd see you lying in bed this late in the day."

His cheek rests on my chest, and I rub his back, enjoying the feel of his warm skin. "I didn't want to leave you." My stomach growls then, embarrassingly loud.

Ian sits up and pats my abdomen. "How about some breakfast? Or, rather lunch."

"Lunch sounds great. And afterward, why don't we visit the marina and check on your boat?"

Ian smiles as he reaches for his sweats. "Really? I'd love that."

"Sure. It's supposed to be a nice day today."

After we dress and eat, we take Ian's Porsche to the yacht club. We park, then walk over to the boardwalk and stroll along the pier out to the berth where Ian's yacht is moored. As we approach the *Carpe Diem,* I feel a sense of *déjà vu.* It's here we met for the second time that first night when I was investigating a murder scene. I guess fate had plans for us.

I can still picture Ian sitting on a wooden crate on the pier, his head hanging between his knees as he battled nausea. I recognized him immediately as the young man I'd seen earlier that night at Tank's. When I first saw him, my heart slammed in my chest, and my body felt like it was waking up after a long hibernation.

Ian pauses at the berth beside his, where his friend Eric's boat was once moored. It's empty now.

I lay my hand on Ian's shoulder. "Thinking about your friend?"

"Yeah. His parents didn't even bother to come for his funeral."

"I'm sorry."

Ian reaches for my hand. "Eric didn't deserve what happened to him."

"No, he didn't." It was a brutal murder.

Just a few yards away, the *Carpe Diem* rocks gently on the dark, murky water. I glance down to see a dead fish floating on the surface, along with lengths of seaweed. The humid air smells of water and fish.

I reach for Ian's hand. "Come on. There's no point in dwelling on painful memories."

We walk the few remaining yards to his boat. Ian steps onto the rear swim platform, and I follow him aboard.

He climbs the stairs to the main deck and does a quick visual sweep of the deck and salon. "Everything looks good."

I can tell he's antsy. Thinking about Eric's death does that to him. "Hey." I pull him into my arms, hoping to distract him. "What d'you say we take the boat out?"

His eyes widen in excitement. "Yeah? You want to?"

"Sure. You said you'd teach me how to pilot this thing. Now's as good a time as any."

He smiles. "Finally, I get to teach you something."

"Why don't you go below and prep the engine? I'll take care of the lines."

He nods. "Sounds good."

As Ian starts to pull away, I hold onto him for just a moment longer. I lean into him and press my lips to his. "I love you."

His smile morphs into a grin. "And I love you."

"All right, go. Let's get this show on the road."

Ian heads below deck to the engine room. While he's doing all the technical stuff down there—checking on fuel and fluid levels and all that—I hop off and loosen the lines securing the boat to the pier.

By the time I'm done and back on board, Ian's already up in the captain's cabin. I join him there, taking a seat in the black leather chair next to his. He starts the engine and checks the weather report.

Ian bought this yacht when he was only twenty-two years old. He'd grown up on his dad's yacht, and he'd always wanted one of his own. He bought this one—a forty footer—and taught himself to operate it on his own. This is his happy place. He feels free and unfettered out on the water.

He backs us out of the berth and heads toward the mouth of the marina. We move at a sedate pace until we pass the no-wake zone, and then he opens up the throttle and we head out into open water.

As a cool wind blows in our faces, I slip my hand into my jeans pocket to check on my wedding band. His band, which is still in its black velvet box, is safely tucked into my jacket pocket. Once we're away from traffic, I'll have him stop and drop anchor. That's when I'll give him his ring.

I enjoy sitting back and watching Ian pilot the boat farther out into the lake. We pass lots of speedboats, jet skis, sailboats, and catamarans, as well as the larger tourist vessels that meander up and down the shoreline. Ian is clearly in his element out here, relishing every moment.

When we're far enough from shore, I tell him to drop the anchor. "Come down to the salon with me. Let's have a drink."

As usual, when we're operating the boat, we forgo alcohol and opt for sparkling grape juice instead. I pull a bottle out of the fridge and pop the cap. Ian grabs two wineglasses from the bar, and I pour us each a glass.

Ian hands me a glass. "What's the special occasion?"

"I'd like to make a toast."

"To what?"

"To us."

His grin deepens. "I'll second that."

We both take sips. Then I lean forward and kiss him, tasting the sweet-tart grape juice on his tongue. I set my glass on the bar and reach into my pocket and pull out the ring box.

Ian's eyes widen the moment he sees it. He stares at the box, then at me. Finally, with a gasp, he sets his glass on the bar next to mine. "Tyler."

I drop to one knee and open the box to reveal his wedding band. The gold shines in the sunlight, and the tiny, embedded diamonds sparkle.

This is a once-in-a-lifetime moment, and I want to savor it. "Ian Alexander."

"Yes?" His voice is shaky as his green eyes fill with tears.

"Ian." Suddenly my mouth is dry. "The moment I first

laid eyes on you, the ground shook beneath my feet. Ever since then, you have filled my dark, lonely existence with light and laughter, and most importantly, with unconditional love. I can't imagine a life without you." I swallow hard and take a deep breath. "Ian, will you please do me the honor of marrying me?"

✑ 10

Tyler Jamison

When Ian covers his mouth with shaking hands, I have to smile. It's not like this is a complete surprise. He knew it was coming. We've discussed marriage, and we picked out our wedding bands weeks ago. But this is *the moment—* the one that truly matters.

"Tyler." Ian's voice cracks. "I can't believe this is actually happening. Oh, my god, yes. Of course, I'll marry you."

I remove the ring from its box, and as Ian holds his left hand out to me, I slip the band on his ring finger. While he stares at his ring, I rise to my feet and fish my own band out of my pocket. He watches with teary eyes as I start to slip it on my finger.

"Wait!" He snatches the ring from me. "Let me do it."

Ian reaches for my left hand, cradling it in his, and slides the band onto my ring finger. Then he brings my hand to his mouth to kiss, his lips grazing my wedding ring. He joins our hands, linking our fingers together. "My husband-to-be." Ian's voice is filled with awe. He glances at our beautiful surroundings—at the open water and the clear blue skies overhead. A cool wind ruffles his hair. "This is the most perfect moment of my life."

My throat tightens at his sincerity. "Mine, too."

Laughing shakily, he dabs at the tears on his cheeks. "I'm such a basket case. When did you pick up the rings?"

"Yesterday, when Layla and Jason came over for an unexpected visit."

Ian gives me a knowing look. "You had them run interference for you, didn't you?"

I nod. "I wanted to surprise you."

Ian laughs again. "Well, you certainly succeeded." He looks down at his ring. "I'm never taking this off. It's a symbol of my love for you."

I reach out to cup Ian's face. "God, I love you. You always know the perfect thing to say." I pull him close. "So, what about the venue? Where are we going to tie the knot? We still have a lot of little details to decide."

"I want something small and intimate," Ian says. "Just family and close friends. Do you think Shane would let us use his Kenilworth house? I can't imagine a more perfect setting."

"I'm sure he'd be happy to." I chuckle. "As my brother-in-law, he can hardly say no."

Ian's eyes light up. "We can ask Cooper to officiate. He's already performed how many marriage ceremonies for the McIntyre clan? Two?"

"Three actually. Shane and Beth's, Jake and Annie's, and most recently Jonah and Lia's."

"That's what I want," Ian says. "For Cooper to officiate. And I want my parents to walk me down the aisle. Aiden can be the ring bearer, and Luke can be the flower boy." He lays his hands on my chest. "And I'd love to see you rocking a traditional black tuxedo. You'll look so debonair."

"Whatever you want." The truth is, he could ask me for anything, and I'd give it to him.

After we finish our sparkling grape juice, we cruise up the shoreline for a couple of hours. Ian lets me sit in the captain's chair, and he shows me how to operate the controls and how to use the radio. He uses his phone to take pictures of our hands and rings. "Ian Jamison," he murmurs with a wistful smile.

"You're taking my name?"

"Of course I am. Why wouldn't I take my husband's name?"

"I assumed you'd want to keep your own name, or maybe hyphenate our names. I'd be okay with that."

Grinning, Ian shakes his head. "No way," he says with absolute certainty. "I'm taking your name."

I lean close and kiss him. "Hello, Mr. *Jamison*."

* * *

After cruising back toward the marina and docking the yacht, we decide to visit our parents to give them the good news.

First, we stop off at my mom's house in the high-security, gated McIntyre compound. The guard on duty waves us through the gate.

I'd already given Mom a heads-up that we were stopping by for a short visit. When we arrive, she opens the front door before I can even knock. "Hello, darlings. Come in. What brings you here?"

Ian holds up his hand and points at his ring. "He did it! He proposed. We're getting married, Ingrid."

My mom throws her arms around Ian's neck and kisses his cheek. "Oh, my sweet boy, I'm so happy to hear this." Then she pulls me into their huddle. "I couldn't be happier. You two are perfect for each other."

When she releases us, her blue eyes shine. "Let me see." She takes both of our hands in hers and studies our wedding bands. "When is the big day?"

"We need to confirm with Shane and Beth," I say. "But we're hoping to have the ceremony at the Kenilworth house."

"As soon as possible," Ian interjects. He grabs my hand and holds it to his chest. "I want to marry this guy before he changes his mind."

I laugh. "As if that would ever happen."

"Come, let's have a drink," Mom says. "We need to celebrate. You can have one drink, can't you?"

After our visit with my mom, we head to Ian's parents' house across town. As we park behind their massive house, we spot Jason's car, which means he and Layla are here as well. Perfect.

We catch them all just as they're sitting down at the dining room table.

"Hey, guys," Ian says as we crash their dinner. He waves his left hand.

Not missing a thing, Layla jumps up from the table, runs to her brother, and throws her arms around him. She grabs his wrist and holds his hand up for their parents to see. "Oh, my god, you guys, look! A ring. It's official. They're getting married."

Ruth is the next one to hug Ian. "Oh, honey, I'm so happy for you both."

Martin joins us, clapping me on the shoulder. "Congratulations, Tyler."

Ian's father and I sure have come a long way since the day he threatened to have me fired from my job as a homicide detective if I continued seeing his son. Fortunately, that's behind us now.

Jason gives Ian a high-five and then shakes my hand. "Congrats, man. I couldn't be happier for you guys."

"You have to stay for dinner," Ruth says. "So we can celebrate. I'll set two more places. Martin, open a bottle of something special, will you?"

* * *

After dinner with Ian's family, we head back to the townhouse to change and get ready for tonight's stake-out at Gina's. As I'm pulling on a pair of jeans, my mind dwells on the nightmare I had last night. It feels like an omen. *A warning.* My gut feels hollowed out.

"I'll be ready in a sec," Ian says as he breezes into the bedroom.

As I sit on the side of the bed, pulling on my socks, I watch Ian disappear into the closet. A moment later, he comes out pulling on a pink T-shirt. It takes me a minute to figure out the design on the shirt—*I want s'more.* It all makes sense when I realize it's a fat marshmallow with a smiley face and a little slab of chocolate sandwiched be-tween two graham crackers.

Ian disappears into the bathroom, and a moment later I hear the water running as he brushes his teeth.

S'mores.

Cute. But not cute enough to dispel my sense of dread. But if I ask him to stay home tonight, he'll hit the roof.

Still, his safety comes first. "Ian."

He waltzes back into the bedroom. "Yeah?"

"You know, it's probably going to be more of the same

tonight. A whole bunch of nothin'. Why don't you stay home? There's no need for both of us to be out all night sitting in a cramped car."

His expression falls, and he looks like a puppy that's just been kicked. "You don't want me to come with you?"

"No, it's not that. It's just going to be another boring night. You could stay here, you know. Relax and watch a movie."

He's staring at me like I just told him I'm moving out. "Ian, don't look at me like that."

"I thought we were partners."

"We are."

"Then why don't you want me to come with you?"

"Just because we're partners doesn't mean we have to do everything together. Sometimes, it'll just be one of us."

"You mean, it'll just be *you* by yourself."

"No, that's not what I meant. Maybe sometimes it'll just be *you*."

Ian rolls his eyes. "Yeah, right."

He plants his hands on his hips. It's clear he's pissed, but he's also hurt. I can see it in his eyes and in the way his lips are on the verge of quivering. His chest rises and falls as he sucks in a breath.

Fuck.

I pull my shoes on and stand. "I'm not trying to exclude you, Ian."

"It sure feels like you are." He storms out of the bedroom and down the hallway. A moment later, he stomps down the stairs.

God, I'm so bad at this. I don't know how to protect him without hurting him.

I pull on my shirt and have it buttoned by the time I reach the ground floor. I can hear him in the kitchen slamming cabinet doors. I need to fix this. I can't bear for him to be hurt or mad at me. What if he decides I'm too much hassle? What if he decides I'm not worth the effort?

I reach the kitchen doorway and watch Ian as he systematically opens and closes half-a-dozen cabinet doors. "What are you looking for?"

He flicks his wrist at me like he's swatting a pesky mosquito. "Go away. I'm busy."

I refrain from laughing as I walk into the kitchen. "Busy doing what, exactly?"

"I'm looking for something."

"What?"

He opens a drawer, blindly reaches inside, and pulls

out a meat thermometer. "This. I've been looking every-where for this."

"You've been looking for a meat thermometer? What are you going to do with it? Stab me?"

He chokes back a laugh as he heads for the patio door. "Don't tempt me, Tyler."

"Ian, stop." When he ignores me, I intercept him before he reaches the door. "Stop, *please*." He tries to pull away from me, but I have a firm grip on his forearm. "I'm sorry."

I wrestle the meat thermometer from him before someone gets hurt and toss it onto the island counter-top. Then I turn him to face me. The hurt in his eyes cuts right through me. "I'm sorry, baby."

When I see him struggling not to cry, I pull him into my arms and hold him close. "Shh," I murmur, my lips pressed against his temple. He's shaking. As I recall Ian's fear of abandonment, his reaction to my request to stay home tonight makes perfect sense. He sees it as rejection.

"You don't want me to come," Ian says in a pained voice.

"No, baby, it's not that. I swear it's not."

"Then what is it?"

"I'm afraid you'll get hurt."

Seemingly caught off guard by my admission, Ian pulls back. "I'm not going to get hurt."

"You don't know that. Either one of us could get hit by a bus anytime we walk out the front door. You never know what's going to happen. You never know when you're going to walk out that door and never come back. It happens, Ian. All the time. No one's invincible."

The corners of his lips turn down. "Oh, my god. Is this about your dad?"

Just hearing him mention my father brings an avalanche of painful memories flooding back. "This has nothing to do with him."

But Ian doesn't look convinced.

He knows my father died in the line of duty, but he doesn't know the details. I don't like to talk about it. It happened over twenty years ago, when I was just out of the police academy. It's an open wound.

Ian stares into my eyes for a long moment as if weighing the truth of my words. Finally, he lays his hands on my chest and smooths the fabric of my shirt. "I'll be really careful, I promise. I'll follow your lead. I'll do whatever you say. Just let me come with you. I want us to do this together. Please, Tyler. This means a lot to me."

I blow out a heavy breath. I know it means a lot to

him. Ian wants to find his place in the world. He wants to be needed, to have a vocation. "All right." I give in against my better judgment.

If anything happens to him, it'll be on me.

* * *

That night, we stake out Gina's for the third night in a row.

Ian gets comfortable in the front passenger seat and sips his coffee. "Thanks for letting me come."

"I'm a shitty boyfriend, aren't I?"

He laughs. "Technically, you're my fiancé now, not my boyfriend. But no, you're not shitty. You're a dreamboat."

Out of the corner of my eye, I notice movement near the café's rear entrance. "Ian. The door."

His gaze follows the direction of mine. There, in the shadows, a slender figure dressed in black approaches the rear door, pulls out a key, and enters the building.

"Oh, my god," Ian says. "It's happening."

I open the center console, pull out my loaded Glock, check the magazine, and tuck the gun into my holster. I glance over at Ian, who's pale as a ghost. "I don't suppose I can talk you into staying in the car."

He practically bares his teeth at me. "Don't even suggest it."

"I was afraid you'd say that. All right, let's go. And for god's sake, please do as I say."

∞ **11**

Ian Alexander

My pulse hammers as I exit the car and quietly close the door. Tyler's already moving across the empty parking lot toward the rear door of the café, and I have to hustle to keep up with him. Following orders like a good soldier, I stay behind him. He's armed. I'm not. Honestly, my job is mostly to stay out of the way and not give Tyler a reason to worry.

Tyler tries the door and, fortunately, it's unlocked. He slowly pushes it open and scans the dark hallway. Gina's office door is ajar, and we see a flicker of light coming from inside, probably from a flashlight. I hear a desk drawer open.

Keeping to the wall, Tyler approaches the office door. He motions for me to stand back, out of the way. When he raises his gun, my heart knocks against my ribs.

Quickly, he peers into the room, then he returns to his position. He holds his finger to his lips, motioning for me to remain silent. Even though my school teachers might have disagreed, I do know how to follow instructions.

With his gun held tightly in both hands, Tyler kicks the door open wide and steps into the room. "Freeze!" he yells in a stern voice that might cause any burglar to wet his pants.

The thief practically shrieks when Tyler flips on the lights.

"Step away from the desk and keep your hands where I can see them," Tyler commands in his sexy cop voice.

"Don't shoot, don't shoot!" pleads a young male. I can't see the kid, but I can tell from his voice that he's not entirely through puberty yet. "I'm unarmed, mister. I swear."

"Ian, call Gina," Tyler says.

I follow Tyler into the room and watch as he frisks

the kid, retrieving a phone and a key ring from the boy's pockets. Tyler sets the items on the desk. "Sit down and keep your hands where I can see them."

The kid sits and glares daggers at Tyler. The brat's pissed because he got busted.

I finally get a good look at the kid, and it's obvious he's strung out. His eyes are wild and glassy, and he's shaking. He looks to be around sixteen.

I call Gina to let her know we caught the thief. "She's on her way," I tell Tyler after I end the call.

Twenty minutes later, Gina shows up, breathless and dressed in sweatpants and a T-shirt. "Ronnie?" she says when she gets a good look at the teenager sitting in her chair.

He keeps his eyes locked on his hands, which are clasped tightly in his lap.

"Apparently, you know him," Tyler says.

Gina nods. "His name is Ronald Stafford, Jr. He's my landlord's son." Exasperated, Gina pulls out her phone and makes a call. "Ron? Sorry to bother you this late at night, but your son broke into my café this evening to steal from me. How soon can you get here?"

As Gina ends the call, the kid hangs his head—either in shame or fear, I can't tell. His scraggly blond hair falls forward to cover his face.

Gina stares hard at the boy. "You're the one who's been stealing from me?" She glances at the key ring lying on her desk. "You stole this key from your dad, didn't you?"

Ronnie doesn't bother to look up.

Finally, we hear the back door open and close.

A moment later, a middle-aged man walks into the office. His gaze goes right to the boy. "Ronnie? What the fuck?" Ronald Sr is dressed in black trousers and a badly-wrinkled white dress shirt. His thinning blond hair is disheveled. It appears he jumped out of bed, threw on yesterday's clothes, and came straight here.

Ronnie doesn't answer his father. He just sits there shaking.

Gina grabs the key ring off the desk and holds it up to the father. "Your son stole a key to this building and has been using it to break into my office and steal cash. This has been going on for *weeks*, Ron."

The landlord looks shocked. "You stole a key from me?" he asks his son.

Ronnie shrugs. "I made a copy."

"And you've been stealing from Ms. Capelli?"

The kid nods.

The father shakes his head in disbelief. Then he turns

to Gina. "I'm so sorry, Gina. I don't know what to say."
He turns back to his son. "How could you do this? How
could you do this to *me*?"

The kid starts crying. "I needed the money."

"For what?" the father asks. "I give you everything you
need. Is this about drugs? Are you using again?"

The kid shrugs.

"How much has he taken?" the man asks Gina.

"About two thousand dollars."

"Are you going to call the police?"

Gina shrugs. "I guess that depends on you. Are you
going to get him the help he needs?"

The father nods. "I will. I swear it. Thank you, Gina.
I'll bring you a check first thing in the morning to re-
place what Ronnie took from you."

After the landlord leaves with his son in tow, Gina collapses into her desk chair. "I never dreamed it was Ron's
son who was stealing from me. Poor Ron. He's a good
guy, and I know he loves his son."

Tyler sits on the edge of Gina's desk. "That kid needs
rehab. I hope he gets help."

Gina nods. "I'll make sure he does."

Tyler and I wait while Gina locks up the café. When
she's ready to leave, we walk her to her car, which is

parked next to the BMW.

It's three-thirty in the morning by the time we reach home. We're both exhausted, so we head straight upstairs to get ready for bed.

I crawl in bed beside Tyler and collapse. "I'm wiped, but I'm also wired."

Tyler laughs. "It's the adrenalin. You'll get used to it." He pulls me into his arms. "So, what did you think about your first criminal case?"

"I hope that kid gets help before he turns into a hardened criminal. It's not too late for him to turn his life around."

Tyler kisses my forehead. "Always the optimist. That's one of the things I love about you."

I roll to face him. "*One* of the things? What are the others?"

His arm snakes around my waist, and he tugs me closer. When his muscular leg slides between mine, my pulse kicks up. "There are so many," Tyler says. "Your sense of humor, your playfulness, your loyalty, your skills in the kitchen. I could go on."

"Please do. What about my skills in the bedroom?"

"Oh, those are legendary." He grips my butt cheek and gently squeezes. "And then there's your ass."

I smack his shoulder. "Be serious."

He grins. "I am." His expression grows serious. "I love everything about you, Ian. Every single thing."

"There's nothing you would change if you could?"

He shakes his head. "Nothing."

"I know I drive you crazy sometimes."

He tightens his hold on me. "I wouldn't change a thing."

Tyler's hand slides up to cup the back of my head as he leans in to kiss me. His lips are hungry, his breath flavored with peppermint toothpaste. I feel every muscle in my body tighten in anticipation.

His fingers dig into my hair as he holds me tightly for his kiss, and that makes me tingle all over. He's bossy and domineering, and it's a huge turn-on for me. He knows it, and I know it.

He lifts my leg up over his hip and presses himself against me. We're both hard now. Every nerve in my body is singing, wanting more. Wanting *him*.

I run my hand up the length of his arm, loving the feel of his rock-hard biceps. My hand moves higher, over his shoulder and up his neck, to cup his face. I brush my palm gently against his soft beard, and with a groan, he closes his eyes.

Tyler turns his face to place a kiss in the center of my palm. Then grasps my hand and draws it down to his erection.

I don't need any other invitation. I stroke him, base to tip, and back again. His response is a harsh moan. I capture our cocks in one hand and begin stroking.

Tyler throws his head back on his pillow, his neck muscles straining, his tendons pulled taut. His breathing grows rougher, his chest rising and falling rapidly as I continue to tease us both. "Oh, god," he groans.

The feel of his cock sliding against mine is mind-blowing. I turn toward him and flick my tongue over his nipple. I take my time as I work us both higher and higher, our flesh hot and hard, both of us aching for release, but also not wanting this to end.

I come first, crying out as my body bucks into the orgasm. Tyler follows right behind me, his hips bucking as he ejaculates. Stroking with long, leisurely movements, I draw out our pleasure.

Like the gentleman he is, Tyler kisses me before he heads to the bathroom to get a wet washcloth. He cleans us up, and when he returns to the bed, I'm so tired I can hardly keep my eyes open.

"Go to sleep," he says as he presses his lips to my forehead. "Tomorrow's another big day."

"Right," I mutter. "Liam's going to kick my ass again."

Tyler laughs as he pulls me close.

ᘓ 12

Tyler Jamison

I have to give Ian credit for trying. He's been working hard all week, having a self-defense session with Liam almost daily. And we've been hitting the shooting range on a regular basis, too, to give him more experience with handguns. He can load a magazine in record time now. And his aim has greatly improved. He can unload an entire magazine of rounds within a four-inch diameter circle.

Right now, Liam is showing Ian how to escape from

being pinned against a wall. It's hard for me to watch Liam slam my boyfriend into the studio wall. It's all simulated, of course, but still it bothers me. It brings home the cold reality that something bad could happen to Ian. It happened to my dad, and he was a twenty-year police veteran. In a single second, he made an impulsive decision to be a hero, and it cost him his life. And it nearly destroyed our family.

If it weren't for Mom's sheer determination to keep her family together, I don't know what would have happened to us. It helped having a newborn in the house. I had a baby sister to help take care of. There was no time for grief.

Liam grabs Ian's throat with one hand and hauls his free hand back as if he's going to punch Ian in the face. Ian traps the hand clutching his shirt, holding it tight to his chest, and with his other hand, he strikes Liam's jaw, shoving his face backward and away, and he ducks out of the path of Liam's incoming fist. Ian then mimics slamming his elbow into Liam's jaw, pulls Liam's head down with both hands, and knees him in the face. While Liam is supposedly recovering from the blow, Ian pulls free.

At least that's how it would happen in an ideal world.

"Excellent!" Liam says as he pats Ian on the back.

"That was fantastic."

Ian looks to me, seeming eager to make sure I'm watching. When I nod my head, Ian beams at me.

"Good work," I say as he jogs over to me.

It looks like he's done for the day. He has a towel slung around his neck. He's sweating, and his hair is matted to his head. "Thanks." Wincing and slightly out of breath, he rotates his left shoulder. "I think I pulled a muscle, though."

Liam joins us. "Nice job, Ian." Then he nods to me. "He's making good progress."

Ian looks so damn proud of himself.

"So," Ian says, grinning at me. "You've been watching me on the mat with Liam for a while now. I think it's time I get to see what *you* can do."

"I'm sure Liam's busy," I say. "He probably needs to get ready for his next class."

Liam checks the clock on the wall. "Actually, I have time. How about it? Want to give Ian a demonstration?"

I glance down at my jeans and sweatshirt. "I'm not really dressed for it."

"Nobody's prepared when they need to defend themselves. It just happens. What are you going to do? Tell them you need to change first?"

Ian bites back a grin. "Come on, Tyler. Please?"

I sigh. "Fine." I step down off the bleachers to follow Liam to the mat. Ian takes my seat, watching eagerly as Liam and I face off.

"What's your poison?" Liam asks as he starts circling me.

I shrug. "Surprise me."

Laughing, Liam nods. "Okay then."

I glance back at Ian, who's watching with great interest. "I hope you're enjoying this."

Without warning, Liam comes at me, hard and fast. I barely manage to get out of his way.

Shit.

I'm a bit rusty. Other than my brawl with Brad Turner a while back, I haven't needed to protect myself in a long time. But I'm not so out of practice that I can't deflect his attack. I duck and pivot, taking the easy way out, then I kick, catching his side as he rushes past.

Liam turns to face me again and nods. "I guess you do remember a few things. For an old guy." Then he turns and winks at Ian.

I can hear Ian laughing across the room.

"You think this is funny?" I ask Ian. But taking my eyes off Liam was a mistake. He barrels into me, knocking me on my back. I roll, getting the upper hand, and pin him to the mat.

A second later, I find myself flipped over onto my back, Liam sitting astride me, pinning both of my wrists to the floor.

I buck upward and knock him off balance. When he falls to the side, I jump up and use a kick to send him flying. Then he's back up, and we're circling each other like a pair of mangy dogs. I'm breathing hard already, but I don't feel too bad about it because he is too.

"Not bad for an old guy?" I ask him.

He smiles just before he shoots a roundhouse kick my way that collides with my side and sends me toppling to the mat. I hit the ground and roll so that I come right back up onto my feet.

Damn.

That hurt.

"I hope you don't bruise easily," Liam says with a grin.

Actually, I probably am going to have bruises.

When he rushes me again, I duck and pivot, managing to get behind him. I put him in a choke hold and pull him back against me. He grabs my arm, loosening my grip, and his foot whips back to trip me. I fall, but I maintain my grip on him, so he falls too. We both hit the ground hard, roll away, and regain our footing. But not for long. I kick out, knocking Liam's feet out from under him, and he goes down hard.

"Ha!" I feel vindicated, but my victory is short-lived because he does the same to me, sweeping my feet out from under me, and I go right down on my ass.

Liam stands and offers me a hand up. "Not bad, Tyler."

"Thanks."

Ian jogs over to join us and throws an arm around me. "That was awesome. You've got skills, babe."

Laughing, I brace myself against his exuberance before we both end up on the floor.

Liam props his hands on his hips and sucks in a lungful of air as he tries to catch his breath. "Like I said, not bad for an old guy."

Ian's grinning like it's Christmas and his birthday all at once. "Yeah, not bad. Not bad at all."

After the workout, Ian changes into his street clothes, and we head to the shooting range for another lesson.

When we walk into the building, Cooper's standing in the lobby talking to some new McIntyre Security recruits. "Hey, guys," he says with a wave.

I point toward the shooting gallery, and he nods. "I'll catch up with you two later."

After putting on ear and eye protection and grabbing a few paper targets, Ian and I enter the gallery and say hi the range supervisor. I step back and motion Ian to walk ahead of me. He finds an available booth and sets his gun case on the floor.

"Go for it," I tell him. "Pretend I'm not even here."

Ian's been shooting enough times now that he should know what to do on his own. There might come a time when I'm not there to help him. He needs to be able to handle his gun on his own.

After hanging a paper target and running it out about twenty feet, he opens my gun case and retrieves my 9mm Glock, an empty magazine, and a box of ammo. I watch silently as he loads the rounds into the magazine and then seats it in the gun.

Ian recently upgraded from the Smith & Wesson .380, and I started him on my gun.

When he glances back at me, I nod. "Go ahead."

Ian turns to face the target. He raises his gun in his left hand—he's a lefty—supports his grip with his right, and lines up the sight. Then he slips his index finger onto the trigger.

Pop, pop, pop. His first three shots go off in rapid succession before he returns his index finger to the safe position, parallel to the chamber. We both look at the target and find three perfect holes within a two-inch radius, dead center.

Damn. He is a good shot.

He looks back at me and grins. "Did you see that?"

"Hell yes, I did. Great job. Keep going." I motion for him to resume.

Ian empties the magazine, refills it, and proceeds to empty that one as well. Almost all of his shots are true, most of them clustered within a three-inch radius dead center.

"Well, damn," says a deep voice behind us. "He's got a good eye."

Ian lays down his gun, and we both turn to see Cooper standing behind us, wearing ear protection.

"He is," I say. Then I nod toward the box of ammo sitting out on the counter. "Load up and go again." Learning to shoot safely is all about developing muscle memory, and that requires lots and lots of practice.

While Ian's loading fresh rounds into the magazine, Cooper says, "Do you guys have plans tonight?"

I shake my head, my attention on Ian as he slams the magazine into the gun. "No."

"Sam suggested we go clubbing tonight. Are you two

interested?"

"Clubbing?" I refrain from rolling my eyes.

But it's too late—Ian already heard him. After laying his gun down, he turns to face us. "We'd love to, right, babe?" he asks, his gaze going to me.

"Sure," I say, unable to resist Ian's pleading grin. How can I say no to that face? "Sounds great."

Cooper nods. "I'll let Sam know."

After gun training, we head for a sporting goods shop to pick up Ian's new handgun. He's already filled out the necessary forms and provided the requisite identification to purchase a gun. His background check has been completed, too. Now it's time for him to select his gun and purchase the necessary supplies.

He doesn't have a concealed carry permit, and I don't think he's quite ready for that. He can own a handgun, but he'll keep it safe at home for now, only taking it out to practice at the shooting range. I do have a concealed carry permit. If anyone's going to carry, it'll be me.

Ian ends up choosing a black Glock 9mm semi-automatic that's well suited for beginners. We buy him ammo, a waistband holster, and a gun safe for him to store the gun in at home.

* * *

Later that night, we meet Sam and Cooper, along with some of Ian's friends, at Sapphires. As usual, Cooper and I end up manning the booth while the young guys hit the dance floor. Being back here makes me a little uneasy. This is where Roy Valdez first set his sights on Ian. And it's where Brad Turner assaulted Ian in the bathroom. But Valdez is dead, and we've never seen Turner here since his assault case against me was adjudicated.

The club is under new management after Valdez's family sold it.

While Sam, Ian, and two of Ian's closest friends—Chris and Trey—are out on the dance floor, gyrating to hot pop tunes under neon blue strobe lights, Cooper and I nurse our beers.

"Ian's a good shot," Cooper says as he sets his bottle down.

Sighing, I nod. Then I take a swig of my beer.

"You don't seem very happy about it," he says.

"I'm not."

"Why's that?"

"I don't like the idea of him being in harm's way. Guns are dangerous things. Even veterans have accidents. I just don't want him to be in a situation where he has to use a gun."

Cooper shrugs. "You have to be prepared for that, Tyler. Just let him keep practicing."

Our server brings fresh bottles to the table.

"Thanks," I tell the young blond wearing tiny leather shorts and nothing else. His muscular chest is smooth and oiled, his nipples pierced. When we're alone again, I turn back to Cooper. "Ian and I would like to ask you for a favor."

"Sure," he says. "Name it."

I hold up my hand to show him my wedding band. "We'd like to ask you to officiate our wedding."

Cooper grins. "I was wondering when you'd get around to asking."

Cooper got licensed to officiate weddings a couple years ago so he could perform my sister's wedding to Shane. Since then, he's officiated at a couple more McIntyre family weddings.

"I've already talked to Shane about letting us hold the ceremony at the Kenilworth house."

Cooper lifts his bottle in a toast. "I would be honored."

I glance at the dance floor, where there's a lot of glistening bare chests, leather vests, and tiny shorts. Dancing couples grope each other openly. I look down at my staid black trousers and white dress shirt. "I stick out like a sore thumb." Then I take in Cooper's red plaid flannel shirt. "So do you. You look like a lumberjack."

Laughing, Cooper nods. "Hey, it takes all kinds."

I'm seated so that I have a clear line of sight to the dance floor. I can't help wanting to keep an eye on Ian. A lot of shit's gone down in the club in the past, and neither one of us is completely over it. Besides, a lot of the guys in this club are drunk, and sometimes they can get a little too grabby. Still, Sam's out there with Ian. He'll be fine.

"You watch him like a hawk," Cooper observes as he nods toward the dance floor.

I don't bother contradicting him. "He's—" I stop what I'm about to say. What? He's fragile? He's sensitive? It's true. He is. His feelings get hurt easily. Finally, I say, "Is it wrong of me to want to protect him?"

Cooper grins. "No, of course not. You wouldn't be you if you weren't overprotective." He sips his beer. "Ian's not helpless, Tyler. Liam says he's coming along nicely in his self-defense lessons."

I nod. "He is. I just hope he never needs to use it."

"If he's going to work with you, it's bound to happen.

You need to be prepared for that."

Grimacing, I shake my head. But before I can say more, all the guys head back to our table.

"I'm thirsty," Ian says as he slides in next to me. He grabs my bottle of beer and takes a swig. Then he makes a face. "Eew. That's awful."

I flag our server, who heads to our table. "Can I get a Cosmo, please?" I ask.

The other guys order a couple rounds of shots.

Ian lays his head on my shoulder and gazes up at me. "You are so good to me."

His expression makes me want to take him straight home and show him just how good I can be.

Before long, our server brings the drinks. Ian finishes his Cosmo and asks for another. Since I drove, he's free to drink. He joins in with Sam, Chris, and Trey as they polish off a flight of Rim Jobs.

"Did you ask him?" Ian whispers to me, loud enough that even the guys at the next table overheard him.

"Yes, I asked him. He said yes."

Ian sits up straight as he looks at Cooper. "You'll marry us?"

"Of course, I will," Cooper says. "I'd be happy to."

"Thank you," Ian says. He tosses back a shot. "Hey,

I know." His gaze bounces from Sam to Cooper. "Tyler can return the favor and officiate *your* wedding! It's only fair, right? Tyler could get licensed. It's not that hard, is it?"

Sam laughs. "No, it's not hard. If they let Cooper do it, they'll let anyone do it."

Cooper elbows Sam.

Ian glances at the ring on Sam's finger. "So, when are you guys tying the knot?"

Sam tosses Cooper a wry look. "Ask him. He's the hold up."

Cooper fidgets, looking a bit uncomfortable being the focus of everyone's attention.

Sam throws his arm across Cooper's shoulders and leans in to kiss his cheek. "We could always elope, babe."

Our server stops at our table to ask if anyone wants anything.

Cooper nods. "I'll take a whiskey. Make it a double."

"Looks like I'm driving home tonight, after all," Sam says, a grin on his face.

Ian lays his hand on my thigh and squeezes. "Any chance I can talk you into dancing with me?"

I lay my hand over his, link our fingers together, and smile apologetically. "Not tonight. Sorry, babe."

"Can't blame a guy for trying." He slides out of the booth, then leans close to kiss my temple. "Come on, guys," he says to his friends. "They're playing my favorite song. Time to dance."

Ian and the others return to the dance floor. As usual, he's the center of attention. I watch as one guy after another tries to join their little party, but his friends do a good job of keeping strangers out of his personal space.

"Tyler," Cooper says, his tone suddenly sharp. "Eleven o'clock. Seated at the bar."

My gaze goes to the spot Cooper indicated, where a dark-haired man sits in the shadows nursing a drink in a glass tumbler. "Son of a bitch."

"Isn't that Brad Turner?" Cooper asks. "I remember him from the courthouse."

From this distance, I can't be sure, but my gut tells me it is. Especially when his gaze drifts from our table to the dance floor.

I haven't had any direct contact with Turner since our day in court. I took a plea deal and avoided both a felony charge and a mandatory prison sentence. I ended up spending only four days in jail. If I hadn't accepted the plea deal, I would have spent a minimum of two years behind bars. Turner didn't get his pound of flesh after all, and I imagine he resents me for it.

My blood pressure is about to go through the roof. I swear to god, if Turner so much as touches Ian, I'll make him regret it.

"He's noticed Ian," Cooper says. "But I don't think Ian has spotted him."

Shit.

Jealousy and resentment are powerful motivators. Turner has made several attempts in the past to hook up with Ian. He's called him. He's even followed him to the marina. He's made it clear that he wants Ian. He's a sick, sadistic monster who gets off on hurting other men. Just thinking about the vile photographs I found when I searched Turner's apartment during my investigation of Eric Townsend's murder turns my stomach.

Ian and the others return to our table, laughing and breathless.

"I gotta pee," Ian says. "Too much to drink."

Ian heads for the public restrooms at the rear of the club. I move to go with him, but Cooper grabs my arm and nods toward Sam, who's already on Ian's tail.

"Relax. Sam's with him," Cooper says. Then he nods toward the end of the bar, where Turner remains seated. "Just keep an eye on him."

"Oh, I'll do more than that." I pull free of Cooper's hold and cross the club. "What are you doing here?" I ask Turner.

He's sitting forward, facing the back of the bar and pointedly ignoring me. He takes a leisurely sip of the clear liquid in his glass, most likely vodka.

"Stay away from Ian," I warn him. "If you so much as speak to him, I'll make you regret it. And stop calling and texting him."

Turner cocks his head as he peers at me. "I have no idea what you're talking about."

"Of course you do."

"No, you're mistaken, *detective*. I've moved on. I have no interest in—*oh, wait*. You're no longer a detective, are you? You were *fired* from your illustrious career like the common criminal you are."

It takes all I have not to haul Turner outside. I spot Ian and Sam returning from the men's room. When Ian catches sight of me standing with Turner, he starts heading toward me, his expression furious. I move to intercept him halfway, grabbing him by his shoulders and turning him toward our table. "He's not worth it."

Ian's livid. "What did he say to you?"

"Nothing." But I can tell Ian doesn't believe me. "It's

time to go."

We return to our booth to say our goodbyes. "It's getting late, guys," I say. "We'd better call it a night."

Cooper meets my gaze. "Good idea. We'll walk you to your car."

* * *

Ian is only slightly inebriated when we arrive home and climb the stairs.

I follow him into our bedroom. "Don't worry about Turner—he's being an ass. Besides that, did you have fun tonight?"

Ian spreads his arms wide and falls back onto the bed. "I did. It was amazing. I just wish you'd danced with me."

"Sorry." I lean over him, caging him in with my arms. "You know dancing in public isn't my thing. But it's yours, though, and you do it really well. I do enjoy watching you."

"Watching can be fun, too." He reaches up to cup my face. "Have I told you lately that I love you?"

Smiling, I nod. "About half-a-dozen times on the drive home."

"Well, I do."

"I love you, too."

His expression grows serious. "I mean it. You're my hero." He threads his fingers through my hair. "You saved me."

"I think it's the other way around."

As he shakes his head, his eyes search mine intently. "I can't wait to marry you, Tyler."

I lean down and kiss the tip of his nose. "You're a little bit drunk."

"Just a little bit. But still, it's true. I can't wait until you're my husband."

As his words tug on my heart, my throat tightens. "I can't wait to be *your* husband." I press my lips gently to his. "My little ray of sunshine."

He smiles at the endearment. "My dark knight."

I'm pretty sure that's a Batman reference. Ian does love his superheroes. But in this case, it's pretty apt. Ian truly is the light to my darkness.

As I skim my gaze down his body, it's impossible to miss the fullness of his erection pressing against the fabric of his skinny jeans. I run my hand down the length of him and smile when he sucks in a sharp breath. He raises his hips, pressing himself firmly against my hand. I can feel the heat of him, throbbing beneath my touch.

I may not be any good to him on the dance floor, but this—this I am good at. I grab the hem of his T-shirt and whip it up and over his head, exposing a lean, chiseled chest. His nipple piercings beckon to me, so I take a moment to tease them gently with the tip of my tongue.

Ian groans and his breathing picks up.

I unsnap his jeans and lower the zipper carefully past his thick erection. His gaze grows hot, and his cheeks flush with arousal. He raises his hips so I can tug his jeans down his long legs.

I love Ian's body. I love looking at him, touching him, and tasting every inch of him. Right now, his erection juts out from his body, thick and demanding. I wrap my fingers around him, marveling at how velvety soft his sheath is, while underneath he's hard as iron.

A glistening drop of precum appears on the tip of his cock. Leaning down, I swipe it away with my tongue.

Ian sucks in a breath as he arches his back, thrusting his hips upward. When I take him in my mouth, all the way to the back of my throat, he cries out, his voice rough. Using my hands and tongue and lips, I drive his arousal higher and higher. He grips my hair tightly, tugging and urging me on. We're both breathing hard now.

"Tyler," he gasps. "I'm—" But before he can speak the

words, he's coming hard and hot, and I swallow every drop.

He's still trying to catch his breath when I lie down beside him, my arm around his waist. I kiss his shoulder, then the side of his neck. I can feel his pulse fluttering against my lips.

He turns to me and, wrapping his arms around me, he buries his head in the crook of my neck. I hold him until his breathing gradually returns to normal.

"I love you," he murmurs sleepily.

I smile into his hair. "I love you, too."

❧ 13

Ian Alexander

We're at home eating lunch the next day when Kimi texts me from the office.

Kimi: Some lady just called asking for Tyler. She sounded frantic.

Ian: We'll be right over.

We scarf down the last of our sandwiches and coffee and leave through the back door, cross the driveway, and enter the office side door. Kimi is seated at the reception desk.

"What's up?" I ask, excited to know we might have another case. I'm still psyched about catching Gina's adolescent thief.

"Some lady called." Kimi frowns as she reads her own handwriting. "She said she's a friend of someone you worked with at the police department." Kimi peers up from the note. "That's you, Tyler."

"Yeah, I figured as much," Tyler says.

Rolling her eyes at Tyler's remark, Kimi resumes reading. "Her nineteen-year-old daughter moved in with her boyfriend, and the mom thinks the boyfriend is abusing her daughter. She—the mom, I mean—contacted the police, and they looked into it, but they said they saw no evidence of abuse. They said the daughter swore everything was fine, but the mom said it's not. She can tell. She said moms know these kinds of things." Kimi pauses to take a breath. "Anyway, she wants to know if you'll look into it."

"Sure," I say. "That sounds easy enough." I glance at Tyler, who looks far from enthused about the idea. "Tyler? We'll take the case, right? I mean, if this guy is hurting that woman's daughter, someone needs to do something about it."

Tyler turns to face me, and I swear he looks like he's about to say no.

I don't understand his reticence. "Tyler? This sounds easy. We go check on the girl, ask her if everything's okay. Easy-peasy, right?"

"What's the mother's name?" Tyler asks, scowling.

Kimi checks her notes. "Marjorie Jones."

"I assume she left her number." Tyler holds his hand out for the info, and Kimi rips off the top sheet of her note pad and gives it to him. Then Tyler nods toward our office. "Let's give Ms. Jones a call."

I follow Tyler into our office, and he closes the door.

"What's wrong?" I ask.

He takes the seat behind the desk. I take the chair across from him.

"Nothing's wrong." But his voice is clipped. Before I can press him for more, he places a call to our potential new client.

"This is Marjorie," a woman's voice says over the speakerphone.

"Ms. Jones, this is Tyler Jamison calling. You're on speakerphone, by the way. My partner, Ian Alexander, is also in the room."

"Oh, thank god, detective," the woman says. The relief in her voice is palpable.

"Actually, I'm no longer a police detective. I'm a private investigator."

"Oh, sorry. Thank you so much for calling. I'm desperate, and the police are no help. I was hoping you'd check on Sydney for me, make sure everything's okay. She told the cops that everything's fine, but I don't believe that for a second."

Tyler grabs a pen and starts taking notes on a pad of paper. "Start from the beginning, Ms. Jones."

"Please, call me Marjorie."

"Marjorie. Start from the beginning. Your daughter, Sydney, is nineteen years old. Is that right?"

"Yes," she says.

"And she recently moved in with her boyfriend. What's his name?"

"Doug Peters."

"And how old is Doug?"

"Twenty-four."

"Can you give me their address?"

As Marjorie rattles off an address, Tyler writes it down.

"And her phone number?" he asks. After he writes it down, he asks her, "Marjorie, why do you think your daughter is in trouble?"

"Because every time 1 talk to her on the phone, she sounds like she's been crying. She texts and talks on the phone, but she won't FaceTime with me anymore. We used to do that all the time. She sounds depressed. She's nothing like her usual bubbly self. I'm seeing red flags everywhere, and 1 need to know if she's okay or not."

Tyler sighs. "All right. We'll do a welfare check on your daughter, Marjorie."

"When? Today? Please, can you do it today?"

When Tyler meets my gaze, 1 nod vigorously.

"Yes," he says. "I'll stop by and see her today."

The woman's voice shakes when she says, "You're a lifesaver, detective. 1 can't thank you enough."

"There's no need to thank me. I'll contact you once we've seen her."

After ending the call, Tyler returns to the front office and asks Kimi to contact the mother to go over the terms of our agreement and pricing information. Then, he nods sharply toward the side door and walks out of the carriage house, leaving me to follow him.

"What's wrong?" 1 ask when we're back in the townhouse. Clearly, something is.

He pours himself a cup of coffee and takes a sip. "You want a cup?" he asks.

"No. I want you to tell me what's wrong."

"Nothing's wrong," he says curtly. Tyler sets his mug down hard on the island countertop. "Ian, I need you to do me a favor. I want you to sit this one out."

I stiffen in surprise. "What?"

"You heard me. I want you to sit this one out. I'll go check on the girl. You stay here."

I stand there for a moment, stunned. I can't believe we're doing this again. "Why?"

"Because I said so," he says, his voice uncharacteristically hard. And then Tyler turns, stalks out of the kitchen, and disappears up the stairs.

My blood starts to boil. We're supposed to be partners in this business. He has no right trying to shut me out. "Don't you dare walk away from me," I yell as I race up the stairs after him.

I find him in our closet, changing out of his jeans and into his black suit—the one he wore to work when he was a homicide detective. "We're supposed to be partners," I say.

"We are," he says brusquely as he buttons his white shirt.

"Tyler?"

"What?" He won't even look at me.

"Tell me what's wrong."

He grabs a black tie off the rack and threads it underneath his collar. His movements are sharp as he ties it. "Nothing's wrong."

Liar. "Then why are you trying to exclude me?"

"I'm not. I just said you need to sit this one out. It's not a big deal. It's just a simple welfare check. You stay home, and I'll take care of it."

"No. I'm coming with you."

Glaring, he turns on me, his expression tight. "Ian." He pauses and takes a deep breath, clearly trying to rein himself in. "This is very likely a case of domestic abuse."

"So?"

"Do you know which types of cases are the most dangerous for law enforcement to respond to?"

"No, but based on the way you're acting, I'm guessing it's domestic abuse."

He nods. "More police officers are killed during domestic disputes than any other type of calls. That's why you're sitting this one out."

"I'm not afraid."

Suddenly, he explodes. "I know you're not, and that's the problem. That's why you're not coming with me. You *should* be afraid."

"You think Marjorie's right, don't you? You think her daughter is in danger."

He nods. "She knows her daughter better than anyone. If she says something's wrong, then something's wrong."

"Well, if it's so dangerous, then I'm definitely coming with you. I don't want you going in there alone. I can be your backup."

Tyler's jaw tightens and his eyes narrow on me. I've never seen him like this before, and it's a bit unnerving. He jabs his index finger in my direction. "You are not coming with me, Ian, and that's final." He stalks out of the closet and back into our bedroom.

As I follow, I try hard to tamp down my hurt. Because this hurts. "I've done everything you've asked me to do to prepare for this job. I've taken self-defense classes, shooting training. I'm sore and bruised from head to toe, and I've never once complained."

I find him sitting on the side of the bed, pulling on his black socks and shiny black loafers. "We're partners, Tyler. Equals. You're not my boss. That isn't how this works."

"Fine. Then I'll call Marjorie Jones and tell her we've changed our minds. We're not taking the case."

"You can't do that!"

His eyes narrow. "Watch me."

I finally lose my shit and explode. "What the hell has gotten into you?"

Tyler shoots to his feet, his expression dark and angry.

My heart hammers in my chest as I try to make sense of this. I can't believe he'd refuse to help someone who might be in danger. "Fine! Then you stay home, and I'll go check on Sydney myself."

Tyler's posture tenses as he stalks toward me. "Oh, hell no." He grabs my shoulders, his grip strong enough to bruise.

I twist out of his grasp and step away, just like Liam taught me. "What in the hell is your problem?"

"I'll tell you what my problem is!" He charges toward me, and I take several steps back until I'm pinned. Tyler slams his fists against the wall on each side of me, caging me in. "You want to know how my father died? I'll fucking tell you how. He died responding to a domestic dispute. Like the fucking hero he was, he stepped between an armed and enraged husband and his pregnant wife, and when the asshole pulled the trigger, he shot my father dead. That's why you're not going with me!"

He grabs my chin firmly and stares hard into my eyes.

"I will not risk your life. I will not lose you, too. Is that clear?" He's seething.

But it's not anger radiating off him in waves—it's fear.

I reach out to cup his face and speak softly. "I'm so sorry about your dad. That must have been awful." I brush my thumbs over his bearded cheeks, gently stroking him like I'm trying to calm down a wounded animal. That's exactly what he is right now—wounded. He's never talked to me about his dad's death, no matter how many times I've asked him.

As tears spring into his eyes, he blinks furiously to clear them. He detests any sort of weakness on his part. My big, strong man isn't allowed to show weakness. Or fear. Or sorrow.

"I'm so sorry," I whisper. When he releases my chin, I lean in to kiss him gently. "I'm so sorry, baby."

He drags me into his arms and holds me so tightly I can barely breathe. He's like a drowning man holding on in desperation.

When he starts shaking in my arms, it takes me a moment to realize he's crying. My heart breaks for him.

Now it's my chance to comfort him. I hold him close and rub his back. "Thank you for telling me about your dad. I can't even imagine how horrible that was for you."

I slip my arms around his waist and press my cheek to his. "It's okay," I whisper. "I've got you."

14

Tyler Jamison

I can't believe I agreed to let him come with me. This is foolish. It's idiotic. And it's dangerous as hell. "Stay behind me, Ian," I say as we approach Sydney's location. "I mean it. And stay alert."

"I will."

We park on the street in front of a rundown apartment building where Sydney Jones reportedly lives with her boyfriend, Doug. The lawn is overgrown with weeds and in desperate need of mowing. There's trash spilling out of dented metal garbage cans lining the side of the building. Children's bicycles and other toys litter the front walk. The building's foundation is crumbling in places.

After making it past all the obstacles strewn across the front walk, we reach the main door, which is hanging on a single hinge. So much for building security. We walk right in.

"Sydney's apartment is on the second floor," I say as I start up the stairs. Ian follows close behind me, saying nothing.

When we reach the second floor, we proceed down a long hallway. The carpet is filthy, stained with god knows what, and there are crayon marks on the dingy walls that might have once been white, but are now yellowed in places.

Sydney's apartment is the last one on the left. Apartment 2G. I knock and wait, but there's no answer. So I knock again. Hopefully, Sydney's at home and Doug isn't. Otherwise, we might have a serious problem on our hands.

Finally, the door opens, but just a crack. The security chain is in place.

A pale female face appears in the slight opening. "Can

I help you?"

"Sydney Jones?" I ask.

She nods warily. "Who are you?"

"Your mom asked us to drop by and check on you."

Her eyes widen, and she shakes her head. "I don't think that's a good idea."

"Your mom is worried about you, Sydney. I promised her we'd make sure you're all right."

"You shouldn't be here," she whispers through the opening. "My boyfriend will be home from work soon."

"This won't take long," I say. "We just want to talk."

She hesitates a moment, as if considering my words. Then the door shuts, and I hear the chain slide free. Sydney opens the door and steps back to let us in.

As soon as I step inside, I immediately note the bruises on the girl's face and neck—both old ones and new ones, including the remnants of a black eye. Her mother's concerns are indeed valid. Ian notices, too. I can tell from his expression as he tries not to stare at the girl.

I do a quick visual sweep of the main room. It's a typical apartment layout, a combined living room and eat-in kitchen. There's one hallway leading toward bedrooms and a bathroom. I motion for Ian to stand back out of the way, and then I close the door behind us.

"You better make this quick," she says as she wrings her hands nervously. "Doug works first shift. He'll be home any minute."

I show her my ID. "I'm Tyler Jamison, and this is my partner, Ian Alexander. We're private investigators. Your mom hired us because she's afraid your boyfriend is hurting you. Based on what I see, I'd say she's right."

Sydney frowns. She hesitates a moment, as if she's debating whether or not it's worth trying to lie to us. Finally, she caves. "I was afraid to tell her the truth because I didn't want to put her in danger. Doug would be furious if my mom knew, and I'm afraid he might take it out on her."

"She says she called the police, and they came to see you, but they didn't find anything."

Sydney bites her lip. "Usually there aren't any visible bruises. Doug's careful that way. But earlier this week, well, he really got mad. He sort of lost it." She points to her face.

"Why was he mad?"

"I told him I want to move back home."

"Do you? Want to move back home?"

Sydney nods. "Yes. You have no idea."

"I think I do. Look, we can help you get back to your

Mom's house right now, but you also need to file a police report so you can get a restraining order against Doug."

She shakes her head. "You make it sound so easy."

"You can't stay here any longer, Sydney," Tyler says gently. "You know it's not safe. It's likely to get worse."

We hear a key rattling in the lock, and then the doorknob turns. A second later, the door swings open and in walks a man wearing dark blue uniform trousers and a matching shirt. His hair is dirty, and his face and hands are marked with grease. He takes one look at me and scowls. "Who the fuck are you?"

I turn to face the boyfriend, my gaze noting that Ian's standing silently behind him, his back against the wall. I don't think Doug has even noticed Ian's presence yet. My heart starts pounding.

"Hey, man, relax," I say, trying to sound friendly. "I just stopped by to say hi to my niece."

Doug's dark eyes narrow on me as he takes a step closer. "You need to get the hell outta my apartment. Right now!"

Out of the corner of my eye, I watch as Ian reaches for the handle of an aluminum baseball bat that's leaning against the wall. Ian grips the handle tightly and lifts it into the air.

Oh, fuck no. I give a quick shake of my head. *Ian, don't.*

"I'm leaving, Doug," Sydney suddenly blurts out, directing Doug's attention to her. "I'm moving back home."

"The hell you are!" Doug yells. He points down the hallway. "Get in the bedroom, bitch. I'll deal with you later."

When Sydney refuses to budge, Doug lunges for her. She ducks behind me. Infuriated, Doug takes a swing at me, just missing my jaw.

Ian's looming closer with that damn bat, so I need to put an end to this right now. I haul off and punch Doug square in the face. He drops like a stone, out cold.

"Grab your stuff," I tell Sydney. "We'll take you home. Ian, call nine-one-one."

"I'm on it," Ian says as he's already putting in the call.

Sydney races off down the hall and returns in minutes with a small suitcase and a backpack. "This is everything."

"Ian, take Sydney and wait in the car," I say as I stand over Doug's unconscious body. "The police will want to get statements from both of you." Then I look pointedly at Sydney. "I suggest you tell them the truth this time." I gesture to the bruises on her face. "I assume there are other bruises besides those?"

She nods. "All over my body."

* * *

As we're pulling away from Marjorie Jones' house, where we left Sydney in her mother's care, I reach over and clasp Ian's hand. "You did good today."

He smiles. "I saw an opportunity, and I was ready to take it. It's what Liam teaches. Look for opportunities. You should have let me hit him."

Laughing, I shake my head. "I didn't realize you were so cutthroat. Maybe next time."

Ian's phone chimes with an incoming text. He reads the message. "Layla and Jason are asking us to meet them for dinner tonight at Tank's. Liam and the rest of the guys will be there."

"Do you wanna go?"

He nods. "Yeah. We can celebrate our win today."

"Then we'll go."

Ian texts his sister back, telling her we'll be there.

We stop at home just long enough to freshen up and change. Tank's is a popular neighborhood sports bar, so we don't need to dress up. I drive, and we park on a side street two blocks from the tavern. When we arrive at six, the place is packed, mostly with locals.

Liam meets us at the door and points the way to a

long table.

Layla jumps up to hug Ian first, then me. She looks relaxed and happy. Her long black hair is up in a ponytail, and she's wearing her favorite burgundy University of Chicago hoodie. Jason stands and shakes our hands.

Already seated at the table are Miguel Rodriguez and Philip Underwood—both employees of McIntyre Security and close friends of Liam. In fact, besides us and Layla, they're all employees of Shane's company.

Layla and Jason return to their seats. They saved two chairs for us. There are already pitchers of beer on the table, along with glasses. Layla, who's a type 1 diabetic, brought her own sparkling water.

While I pour beers for myself and Ian, Liam hands us menus.

A curvy brunette with short, curly hair brings a bouquet of half-a-dozen helium balloons to the table, which she presents to me and Ian. "You two must be the happy couple," she says with a grin. "What can I get you to eat?"

The balloons are clearly wedding themed. One says *Congratulations!* Another has a pair of wedding rings, one has a pair of champagne glasses, two of them say *MR*, and one says *Happy Ever After.*

After we place our food orders—mostly burgers, hot

wings, and loaded nachos—our server heads to the kitchen.

Layla lifts her water bottle. "Cheers to the happy couple!"

They all raise their glasses to join in the toast.

"It's a bachelor party," Ian says, grinning as he leans into me. Under the table, he squeezes my thigh.

I take a sip of my beer. "You don't say."

The wedding is just around the corner. Since it's a small, family event, we've kept everything pretty lowkey. This little impromptu celebration comes as a complete surprise to both of us.

"So, whose idea was this?" Ian asks.

"Mine," Layla says. "My brother's getting married. Of course we have to celebrate."

Ian blushes. "You guys shouldn't have." But his grin says everything. He's touched. We both are.

"I'm so happy for you," she says, her eyes tearing up.

"Thanks, everyone," Ian says. He reaches for my hand. "We really appreciate it."

Our food comes soon, and everyone digs in. While we're eating, I tell everyone what Ian almost did at Sydney Jones' apartment.

Liam reaches across the table to fist bump Ian. "That's

my protégé. I'm proud of you, buddy."

While everyone eats and drinks, conversation flows around the table.

I sit back and observe, watching Ian with his friends and sister. It's hard to believe that in just a week's time, we'll be married. All that's left to do is apply for the marriage license, and then Cooper will officiate our ceremony at Shane's estate north of the city.

Before we know it, Ian and I will be joined, not just emotionally, but legally as well. The idea fills me with a tremendous sense of satisfaction. Knowing he'll be mine, knowing he *wants* to be mine, blows my mind.

That night, as we're lying in bed, I ask Ian, "So, have you decided where you want to go for our honeymoon?" I really don't care where we go. As long as we're together, I'll be happy.

He rests his chin on my shoulder. "I want to go somewhere warm and sunny, with beaches and palm trees."

I laugh. "Well, you're not going to find that around here, not this late in the year."

"How about Key West?" he suggests. "We could fly down and spend a week lazing in the sun."

"Warm weather and sunshine sound good to me. Can we get reservations on such short notice?"

"I can." Ian starts drawing lazy circles on my chest. "Besides, the crowds have thinned out this late in the year, so we should be fine. I'll start making calls tomorrow. We just have to decide what we want—a resort or something more private, like a villa on the beach."

"Well, you know what I'd pick if it were up to me. Something quiet and secluded. But I'll go along with whatever you want."

Ian grins. "How about an exclusively gay resort?"

"That sounds... really festive." I groan. Ian likes pushing me out of my comfort zone. "Okay. Whatever you want, baby."

It'll be a small price to pay to make him happy.

⌕ 15

Ian Alexander

Today's going to be a busy day. There's still a lot to be done in preparation for our wedding this coming weekend. After breakfast, Tyler and I head to the Cook County Clerk's office to apply for our marriage license. We take a number and wait in line with all the other couples. I'm glad to see we're not the only same-sex couple applying for a license. Two women are applying as well.

After the clerk hands our license to Tyler, he hands it

to me. My heart skips a beat when I see our names printed on the certificate.

Tyler Jamison

Ian Alexander

We have an official marriage license.

It's for real, completely legit, and I feel utterly overwhelmed. I could pinch myself.

As we drive away from the county building, I can't
stop staring at the piece of paper in my hand. I just keep
reading our names over and over. Tyler's gaze is on the
road for the most part, but I catch him casting glances
my way. I'm not sure if he's looking at the license or at
me.

"You okay?" he finally asks, sounding more curious
than anything.

I clear my tight throat. "Oh, my god, yes. I'm more
than okay. I'm—I can't even put it into words. When I
was a kid, opportunities like this didn't exist for same-
sex couples. I assumed I'd never be able to get married."

Tyler looks pensive as he watches the road. "To be
honest, I never expected it either."

I know Tyler struggled with his sexual identity for a
long time. Until he met me, he only dated women, and
no matter how hard he tried, it just wasn't working for

him. "I'm surprised you didn't just settle down and marry a woman."

"I thought about it. A lot. I came close to proposing once, but I couldn't go through with it. It didn't feel right to saddle a woman with a husband whose heart really wasn't invested in the relationship. Not like hers was. So, I resigned myself to being a lifelong bachelor."

My heart breaks for all the lonely years he endured. I lay my hand on his thigh. "I'm glad you waited."

He smiles at me. "So am I. *You* are worth it."

I nearly choke up. "Now you're just sweet-talkin' me."

When I glance forward, out the front windshield, I notice we're in Lincoln Park, Tyler's old stomping grounds. He drives slowly down Armitage Avenue, past a row of quaint shops, until he parks in front of one called *The Black Tux.*

"This looks good," he says.

The front windows are filled with mannequins dressed in stylish tuxedos. My pulse flutters when I imagine Tyler in one of them. Just picturing it makes me weak in the knees. He's a handsome man, and he looks amazing in a suit. But put him in a tux, and oh, my god. I can't even imagine the swoon.

Tyler opens the door for me, and I step into a classy,

well-lit storefront. Inside, the shop is clean and tidy. The floors are a polished light wood, and the walls are whitewashed. There are a few racks of men's tuxedos, stacks and stacks of white dress shirts laid out on wooden tables, racks of ties, and another rack of shiny black Oxfords.

A silver-haired sixty-something comes to greet us. "Can I help you gentlemen?" His face is weathered and wrinkled, but he carries himself with a dignified air. He looks us both over. "So, who's the lucky man?"

Tyler and I both say, "I am."

The salesman raises an eyebrow at us, but his expression remains neutral. "What can I do for you?"

"I need a tux," Tyler says.

"What were you thinking of?" the man asks.

"How about a black jacket, gray vest, and a pinstriped tie," I suggest.

Ted looks from me to Tyler.

Tyler nods. "Whatever he says. And I need it this weekend. Is that a problem?"

"Well, no," the man says with a hint of hesitation. "Not if we can find something off the rack." The salesman grabs a tape measure and takes some basic measurements. "I think I have something that will fit you nicely. Follow me, please."

Ted—that's his name, according to his nametag— moves down a wall of clothing racks and selects a pair of black trousers, a white dress shirt, a black tuxedo jacket and a soft gray vest. "How about trying these on for starters? Just to get the sizing." He motions Tyler toward a black curtain. "You can change in there."

While Tyler takes the items into a changing room, Ted invites me to take a seat on one of the brown leather chairs positioned outside the changing rooms. But I'm too antsy to sit, so I end up pacing instead. I scan a rack of ties and select the perfect one.

I hear the rustle of fabric coming from behind the curtain as Tyler changes. My pulse speeds up as I anticipate the big reveal when he walks out of that changing room.

It seems like he's taking forever, but admittedly, he has a lot to put on.

When the curtain is finally pulled aside and Tyler steps out, my breath catches in my chest. "Oh, my god."

He stands facing me, his arms stretched out to his sides. "Will this do?"

My jaw is hanging open. "Will it do? Are you kidding me? Have you even looked at yourself?"

I turn him to face a large, gilded mirror. "Babe, you

look incredible."

The tuxedo jacket fits him perfectly, as if it were tailored.

I hand Tyler the tie. He slips it around his collar, and I tie it for him and then step back to take it all in. He looks stunning.

When Ted clears his throat, I glance back just in time to see the old guy looking flustered.

No kidding, mister. Tyler's hot as hell.

"That looks quite good on you, sir," Ted says. He sounds like a butler. "How's the fit?"

Tyler turns back to face the mirror. He stares at himself, turning to the left, then to the right. He flexes his arms and shoulders. "It feels good." Then he looks at me. "Do you like it?"

I nod. "Seriously, you're a god."

Tyler grins, then tells Ted, "I'll take it."

"Will you be needing shoes?" the sales guy asks.

"No. I've got shoes. Just the tux, shirt, and tie."

"And what about you, young man?" Ted asks me after Tyler returns to the dressing room to change back into his own clothes. "Shall we see if we can fit you as well?"

I stand. "Nope. I haven't decided what I want to wear yet, but it's going to be something absolutely amazing."

Ted smiles. "I don't blame you."

* * *

I ask Beth to go shopping with me to find my wedding outfit. She always looks amazing, and I know she'll help me pull off my vision. I don't want to wear a traditional black tuxedo. Quite the opposite. Tyler is my dashing hero—literally tall, dark, and handsome. I want something different.

When I called to ask if she'd mind coming with me, Beth squealed over the phone. "Oh, my god, yes! I'd love to help you."

So, Tyler drops me off at the apartment building, and I ride up in the private elevator to the penthouse. Beth is waiting for me in the foyer when the elevator doors open. She looks amazing in a pale blue linen dress. She's holding her newborn daughter in her arms.

"Hi," I say, a bit breathless from excitement.

"Tyler's not coming up?" she asks when she sees I'm alone.

"No, just me. I don't want him to see what I'm wearing until the ceremony. It's bad luck."

Beth grins. "This is so exciting."

Sam joins us in the foyer, holding Luke propped on his hip. "Hey, Ian. You excited?"

"You have no idea."

Beth starts for the door to the foyer. "Let us hand the kids over to Rachel so we can go."

When they return, the three of us take the elevator down to the parking garage. Sam's coming with us as Beth's bodyguard, of course. But he's also coming along as my friend. Beth's driver, Joe, is waiting for us in the Escalade, which is idling just outside the elevator.

Sam climbs into the front passenger seat, and Beth and I sit in the back.

"So, what are you looking for?" Beth asks me.

"Something amazing. Something white, or maybe off-white. I'm no virgin, of course, but I still want to wear white on my wedding day."

Sam grins. "Are you sure you're not a virgin?"

I lean forward and smack his shoulder. "Hardly."

"So, what are you thinking of?" Beth asks. "A suit? A tux? What?"

"I'm not sure. Maybe a white tuxedo."

"I know just the place," Beth says. She recites an address to Joe.

When we arrive at a nondescript strip mall, Joe drops

us off at the front door of a men's clothing shop. The location doesn't look very promising, but as soon as we step inside the doors, I know we're in the right place. Everywhere I turn, there are racks and racks of gorgeous suits and tuxes, all organized by color. Black, gray, white, cream, pastels, jewel tones. Linens, silks, and satins. Ties and vests and cummerbunds of every color imaginable.

I head right for the rack of white tuxedos.

"What's your size?" Beth asks.

I rattle off my measurements, and we all start sifting through the selection.

Beth pulls a jacket off the rack. "How about this one?"

She's holding up a soft-white tuxedo jacket with wide satin lapels. "Please tell me it's my size."

She checks the label. "You're in luck."

Sam holds out a pair of matching men's slacks. "Here you go, Cinderella. Try them on."

I grab a white dress shirt, the jacket and trousers, and I'm literally shaking as I carry the garments into a changing room and try them on. When I come out from behind the curtain, Beth and Sam are waiting for me.

Beth beams at me. "Ian, you look beautiful."

Sam nods approvingly. "Tyler's going to swoon when he sees you."

I turn in a circle, my arms out to my sides to give them the full effect. "Do you think he'll like it?"

"He'll love it, Ian," Beth says.

Sam nods. "It's perfect. You look freaking amazing, and Tyler's going to love it."

"Now the tie," Beth says. "What type do you want?"

"I was thinking I'd go with a bow tie, just to be different." I move over to the rack of ties and scan the offerings, looking for my favorite color.

Sam snags a teal one. "Here you go."

I take it from him and hold it up to my neck. "How does this look?"

Beth comes up behind me and slides her arm around my waist. "It's perfect."

After I purchase my tux and accessories, we head back to the penthouse to let Beth and Sam out. Joe kindly offers to drive me home.

Before she opens the car door, Beth pulls a package out of a sack sitting on the floor at her feet. It's wrapped in white paper with delicate gold curlicues and addressed "To the happy couple."

"Can I open it, or should I wait for Tyler?"

"Go ahead and open it," she says. "I'm dying for you to see them."

I unwrap the package and open the lid to a square box. Inside are two matching coffee mugs nestled protectively in white tissue paper. I lift one out and see that it has the words *tyler + ian* printed on it in a charming handwritten font.

She smiles through teary eyes. "I know how much you two love your morning coffee."

"Beth, thank you." I dab at my eyes. "You're going to make me start crying."

Sam laughs. "Start? I have news for you, pal. The waterworks have already started."

I put the mug back in its box and throw my arms around Beth. "You're the best sister-in-law I could ever imagine." And then I hug Sam, too, for good measure.

After Beth and Sam step into the private elevator that will take them up to the penthouse, Joe very kindly offers to drive me home. I move to the front passenger seat.

"Congratulations on your upcoming wedding," Joe says as we leave the parking garage. "I know Ms. Ingrid is absolutely over the moon that her boy is gettin' married and she's gaining you as a son-in-law."

I smile at the compliment. "The feeling is mutual, believe me. Ingrid is an amazing woman."

"Indeed she is," Joe says as he fights a smile.

I'm tempted to ask him to expound upon his opinion of Tyler's mom, but I shouldn't pry. But it's kind of obvious that he has a thing for Ingrid, and I suspect the feeling is mutual. I've seen the way she looks at Joe when he's not watching her. And I've seen the way he looks at her. I guess you're never too old for a second chance at romance. "Have you told her how you feel?"

Joe's head snaps to me. "Excuse me? What in the blazes are you talkin' about, son?" He honestly looks like he has no idea.

"Never mind." I shrug. I guess they'll have to work this out on their own.

My phone buzzes with an incoming message. I grab it and check the screen, expecting a message from Tyler. But it's not. It's from *him*. Brad.

Unknown Number: We need to talk. Let's meet at ur boat

I'm having a flashback to the last time Brad asked to meet me at my boat. He's obsessed with the idea of us hooking up on my yacht, just like he did with Eric on Eric's boat. Brad is a sadist, and I'd die before I ever let him touch me.

Ian: Go to hell

Unknown Number: already there, thanks to u and ur asshole boyfriend. U owe me. Meet me this afternoon @ 3

Ian: Are u insane? I'm not meeting u

Unknown Number: You'd better

"Everything all right?" Joe asks when I shove my phone back into my pocket.

"Yes, fine."

"It doesn't look fine, if you don't mind me sayin'. You look like you've seen a ghost."

I laugh. "You've got that right." *A ghost.* That's exactly what it feels like. Brad Turner is looking for his pound of flesh. He didn't get the revenge on Tyler that he wanted, so now he's trying a different tact.

I need to tell Tyler that Brad is still texting me, but I'm afraid of how he'll react. The last time Brad came after me, Tyler came to my rescue and got himself arrested in the process for assaulting Brad. He nearly went to prison because of it. I can't imagine how he'll respond this time.

* * *

"You're really not going to show me?" Tyler asks that night as we're getting ready for bed.

Tyler showered before me, so he's already in bed, sitting up and leaning against a stack of pillows propped against the headboard. He's reading on his tablet—probably something boring. He's got his reading glasses on, which is sexy as hell.

I shake my head. "No. It would spoil the effect. You can't see what I'm wearing until the ceremony. Besides, it's bad luck."

He lays his tablet on the nightstand. "If you insist."

I climb onto the bed, kneeling as I lean close to kiss him. "I do."

Tyler pulls me onto his lap so that I'm straddling him, and immediately I feel his erection nudging me through the bedding. His gaze goes to my nipples, and he gently draws circles around my areolas, sending violent shivers through my body. "I mean, if you're sure," he says.

I laugh. Now he's just teasing me.

"Is it teal?"

Grinning, I bite my lip. "Not exactly."

"What does that mean?"

"You'll have to wait to find out." He loves to tease me about all the teal I wear. "Don't make fun of teal. You know it makes my eyes pop."

"How about a hint?"

I slip his glasses off and set them aside. Then I lean down and kiss him, hoping to distract him from this line of questioning. He's a master interrogator. "No more hints. I've already said too much. I will say, though, that your sister is a lifesaver. She totally got the look I was going for."

Tyler groans. "These wedding preparations are endless. I'm starting to wish we'd just gotten married at the courthouse."

I swat his bare shoulder, which is impressively rock hard. "Don't you dare say that. It's fun. And it's coming together in record time. Most couples take *months* to plan their weddings, sometimes years, but we're doing it in little over a week."

Tomorrow we're meeting with Gina Capelli to finalize the catering, including the wedding cake. After that, we have an appointment with the florist. Then almost everything's done.

"You can make it until Saturday," I tell Tyler, rubbing myself against his erection.

He groans. "Fine." His hands slide behind me to grip my butt cheeks and squeeze lightly. "In the meantime, I know how you can distract me."

I rock my hips against his. "What did you have in mind?"

* * *

Later, as I'm about to fall asleep, I check my phone one last time for new messages from Brad, but there aren't any. Thank god. I don't want this escalating. I wish Brad would stop obsessing over us and move on.

I put my phone on silent and lay it on my nightstand. When I roll closer to Tyler, he automatically tucks me close to him. Sighing deeply, I allow myself to relax and fall asleep in his arms.

༄ 16

Tyler Jamison

The next morning, Gina Capelli greets us at her coffee shop with open arms. "I can't thank you two enough. Ronnie Stafford is in rehab, and his father reimbursed me for all the money his son took, plus interest. I'd say it's a win-win. We got our money back, and Ronnie will hopefully get the help he needs."

"I'm just glad we could help," I tell her.

"Now, let's talk about something far more pleasant. Let's go taste your appetizers. And then I'll give you a sneak peek at your wedding cake."

We already gave her a list of the hot *hors d'oeuvres* we want for our wedding reception, as well as the flavor and decorations we want for our cake. Today, we get to taste samples of everything.

Like the consummate professional she is, she already has little plates set out on a table for us, each one holding samples of the *hors d'oeuvres* we ordered. And in the center of the table is a miniature wedding cake, a small, single-layer round cake.

"Have a seat, gentlemen," she says, motioning toward the waiting chairs.

We sit, and she takes the third seat. She has a clipboard in front of her and is holding a pen.

"Let's have you taste each *hors d'oeuvres* and tell me what you think. If you don't like something or want to make a change, just tell me. It's no problem at all. Lastly, I'll have you taste the cake." She grins at us. "We'll save the best for last, and I think you'll really like it."

Ian and I work our way through the appetizers, one at a time, and give our feedback.

"Ohmygod, this is so good," Ian moans as he takes a bite of a miniature savory tart.

Gina smiles, then looks to me as I have a taste. "And

you, Tyler? What do you think?"

I take a bite and chew. "I think it's fantastic."

We try a variety of finger foods, everything from little quiches to salmon-and-cream-cheese pinwheels, meatballs, chocolate-covered strawberries, and a half-dozen other finger foods.

"Gina, these are all fantastic," Ian says as he sneaks another chocolate-covered strawberry. Then he looks at me. "Right, babe?"

I nod as I chew. Honestly, I'm not surprised that each one is perfect. Gina is a brilliant caterer.

Then comes the cake. We chose a vanilla pound cake infused with almond extract. The white icing is a cream-cheese concoction. The edging is pink strawberry-flavored piping decorated with gold-foil leaves and fresh strawberries.

Gina cuts us each a slice and hands them to us on little plates. Then she hands each of us a fork.

Ian is the first to dig in. He cuts off a large piece of his slice and pops it into his mouth. His subsequent moan says everything. "Ohmygodyes."

Smiling, I take a bite. Yeah, it's good. Really good.

"This cake is amazing, Gina," Ian says as he cuts off another piece. Then he looks to me. "It's good, isn't it? I told you it would be."

I nod. "Right." To be honest, I don't care what we eat at our wedding. This is all for Ian because he has this vision in his head of what our wedding should be. I just want us to say *I do*. I'm more interested in the end result. I'll let him sweat over the process and the details.

Everything turns out to be perfect, which doesn't surprise me at all. This is Gina Capelli we're talking about. She comes from culinary royalty, so I knew everything would be amazing.

After we give Gina our approval, Ian hugs her, and we say our goodbyes.

Next, we're off to the florist to pick out the flowers. That turns out to be even easier because Ian knows exactly what he wants—teal calla lilies paired with cream roses. He orders matching corsages for the mothers and our sisters, boutonnieres for us and for Ian's father, and a half-dozen bouquets to decorate the room.

I just sit back, relax, and watch Ian do his thing. He knows exactly what he wants, and that's fine with me.

* * *

That night, we order a pizza, pop open some bottles

of beer, and kick back on the sofa to watch the newest Spiderman movie.

"You're awfully quiet tonight," I say. "Is something bothering you?"

We're lying on the sofa, both on our sides. I'm in the back, and he's in front of me. His ass is tucked nicely against my groin, and I know he can feel my erection, because he keeps pressing back against me. My arm is around his waist, and he links our fingers together.

While he's engrossed in the movie, my attention is on him. This right here—something so simple as watching a movie together—means everything to me. I lived so long without this, craving this kind of connection. Now that I have it, I realize the only fear I have is losing it.

I release his hand so I can stroke his arm, from shoulder to wrist and back again. I love feeling the contours of his lean muscles. As I run my fingers up his shoulder, to his neck, a shiver runs through him, and he groans as he tilts his head back. I kiss the back of his head, nuzzling his hair. Then I cup his throat, my fingers gently spanning his neck.

Arching back, he groans again, this time the sound deeper in his throat, harsher. He's breathing harder now, and his attention has shifted from the movie to me. I feel him swallow hard, the tendons in his neck tightening.

"Do you want to finish watching the movie?" I ask. If he does, I'll wait. I can be patient.

He reaches back to grasp my hip and pulls me closer. "What movie?" he breathes.

I smile. *My baby is hot and bothered.* "Then what do you want?"

"You."

I slide my hand down his chest and slip my fingers up beneath his T-shirt. Unerringly, my fingers find his nipples, and I tease them gently, just the way he likes, flicking and pinching, then circling my finger around the flat disk. His hips start moving then, rhythmically pushing back against me, and that only makes me harder and the ache worse for both of us.

"Are you ready to marry me?" I ask him, my voice low and rough.

He sucks in a breath. "God, yes."

"You want me to be your husband?"

He groans. "Tyler— "

"What?"

Another groan, this one more plaintive. "Stop torturing me."

"Am I torturing you?"

"Yes! You know you are."

"Do you like it?"

With a frustrated groan, Ian rolls off the sofa, kneeling on the rug, and turns to face me. His mouth crashes against mine, and he kisses me hungrily. He threads his fingers through my hair, tugging sharply and pulling my mouth closer to his. Then his hand slides down my arm, to my hips, and without breaking eye contact, he tugs open the fastener on my jeans.

"I'm taking you upstairs," I tell him.

"You'd better. But first, I want this."

As he lowers my zipper, I raise my hips and tug down my jeans. And then I'm the one groaning, harsh sounds coming from my throat as I throw my head back on the cushion. And then his mouth is where I need it, enveloping me in wet heat. He teases me mercilessly, tugging and sucking until I'm thrusting mindlessly. His warm hand slips between my legs, and he gently massages my sac. I dig my fingers into his hair and let the storm surge through me.

After I come back down to earth post-orgasm, I stand and adjust my clothing. I take Ian by the hand and lead him upstairs to our bed, where we take our time with each other.

* * *

The next day, while Ian is visiting his sister, I head downtown to Shane's office building. There's something I need to ask him, but I've been putting it off. The truth is, I'm afraid he might say no.

Shane and I have had our problems in the past. I did have him arrested and thrown in jail simply because I was pissed at him. It was, admittedly, a shitty thing to do. I let him out in less than twenty-four hours, but the damage had already been done. Not only did I screw him over but I hurt my sister in the process. I should never have let my anger—and my fear for Beth's safety—get the best of me.

My brother-in-law's office is located on the twentieth floor of his office building. I take an elevator up and find his admin, Diane Hughes, watering some potted trees in the executive lobby. "Hello, Diane."

She pauses to give me a frosty look. Apparently, she still holds a grudge against me for daring to arrest her precious boss. "Detective Jamison. What can I do for you?"

"Call me Tyler, please. I no longer work for the Chicago PD."

Her expression softens, and I see a flicker of remorse in her light blue eyes. "I'm sorry, I forgot. My apologies, Tyler. Old habits are hard to break. How can I help you?"

I glance toward Shane's door, which is closed. He usually keeps it open when he's available for walk-ins. "I was hoping to talk to your boss. It looks like he's in a meeting."

She smiles. "He's on the phone with Beth. Heaven forbid those two go an hour without speaking." She smiles. "Go right in. I'm sure he won't mind."

"Thanks." I cross the lobby and knock.

"Come in!" Shane says.

I crack open his door enough to stick my head through the opening. "Got a minute?"

"Sure." He waves me in. To my sister, he says, "Tyler's here, sweetheart. Can I call you back?"

I walk inside and close the door behind me. Then I take a seat in front of his desk.

"What's up?" he asks.

I can't help smiling. I'm having a serious case of *déjà vu* at the moment. This reminds me of how our story started. I came to Shane's office one day to enlist his help in keeping Beth safe when I learned that the monster who'd abducted her was being released early from prison.

"What's so funny, Tyler?"

I motion between us. "This. Does it remind you of anything?"

He smiles. "We've come a long way, haven't we?"

"I should say so. I guess I owe you a blanket apology for being an ass to you in the beginning."

"It's okay. I don't blame you. You were just protecting your sister. I approve."

I glance at the wall behind Shane's desk, where photographs of him and Beth, their kids, and the four of them hang. He also has framed pictures of them sitting on his desk. No matter where he looks in his office, he sees reminders of his family. My family, too.

I look him directly in the eye. "I have a favor to ask."

He nods. "Of course. What do you need?"

"Ian and I appreciate you letting us use your house for the wedding."

"It's our pleasure." He's including Beth in that as well. Technically, that property is half hers since they're married.

I blow out a breath. "Liam and Miguel and the rest of the guys are going to be Ian's groomsmen. I was wondering if you would stand up with me, as my best man."

I can tell from his expression that I caught him off

guard. Finally, he grins. "Really? You're asking *me*?"

"Yes, really. You know I don't have a lot of friends. But you and I, we have history. You've become an important part of my life, so I thought—"

"I would be honored, Tyler. Thank you."

"That was easy."

He laughs. "See? I'm not a difficult guy to get along with. We're family."

✑ 17

Ian Alexander

The night before the wedding, I pack a small suitcase, grab my wedding garment bag, and head to Liam's apartment around eight. He lives in the same building as Beth and Shane. So do Sam, Miguel, and Philip, who join us. My friends Chris and Trey come, too. All my groomsmen are here. We're having a bachelor slumber party.

We order in food for a late dinner and watch a popular horror movie, which turns into a drinking game. Every time a character screams or dies, we all down a shot. We limit ourselves to beer because there's a lot of screaming and dying in this movie, and we don't want crushing hangovers in the morning.

As I look around the living room at these guys who've become my friends, I realize how much Tyler has brought to my life. Liam, Sam, Miguel, Philip—all of them mean the world to me now. They've accepted me, as well as my friends Chris and Trey, with open arms.

"So," Trey says, looking around. "No male strippers tonight?"

I laugh. "Sorry, no. It's not that kind of party."

Chris laughs. "I don't think all these straight boys could handle male strippers."

The movie is a hoot, and I'm already getting a nice little buzz. Most of us are piled onto the sofa. Trey and Miguel are sitting on the floor at our feet. Their job is to replenish our shot glasses each time we take a drink. They're pretty busy.

Horror movies are always funny when you're half-smashed. The only thing missing is my husband-to-be. I wish he was here, but part of the fun of spending the night before our wedding apart from each other is the anticipation of seeing him again tomorrow, at the altar, dressed in our wedding finery. I can't wait to see him in his tux, looking all handsome and serious. I get goosebumps just thinking about it.

When my phone chimes, I check the screen, hoping it's a message from Tyler. Yes! It is.

Tyler: Do you miss me yet?

I ignore the movie long enough to text him back.

Ian: I miss you to death. What are you doing?

Tyler: Reading and wishing you were here. The house is way too quiet when you're gone.

Swoon. He always says the most romantic things, even when he isn't trying.

Sam tosses a pillow at my head. "Ian, get off the phone! You're going to miss the good part."

"Yeah, quit texting your boyfriend," Liam says.

"He's not my boyfriend. He's my fiancé."

Ian: gotta go, babe. Talk later. Love u.

Tyler: Love you too. Behave.

Part of me focuses on the movie, but another part of me is mentally back home with Tyler, wishing I could cuddle with him on the sofa while he's reading. *Parting is such sweet sorrow.*

I redirect my attention to the TV screen just as a girl

walking alone in the dark woods gets jumped by a bad guy. She screams, and we all take a swig of our beer. I'm having fun, but I'd be having more fun if Tyler was here. For a second, I consider asking the guys if they'd mind if Tyler joined us, but then that would defeat the whole purpose of spending the night away from him. I'll see him tomorrow afternoon, when we're ready to speak our vows. I guess that will have to do.

My phone vibrates again with an incoming message, and I smile as I sneak a peek at the screen. But it's not from Tyler.

Unknown number: u stood me up

Ian: go to hell

Unknown number: ur going to regret this

Ian: LEAVE ME ALONE!!!!!

Unknown number: I'll make him pay

My stomach drops, and my chest tightens.

Sam lobs a sofa pillow at my head. "Seriously, Ian, do I have to confiscate your phone? You'll see Tyler tomorrow. You two can survive being separated for one night, can't you?"

I stare at my phone, feeling sick. "It's not from Tyler."

Sam's demeanor suddenly changes. "What's wrong?"

"I'm not sure."

Sam leans over and grabs my phone, then skims the text thread. "Who's this from?"

Liam takes my phone from Sam, reads the messages, then hands the phone to Miguel, who does the same.

Miguel looks at me. "Is that from Turner? What an asshole."

I nod. "He's been messaging me for days."

"Does Tyler know?" Sam asks.

I nod.

Sam frowns. "Screenshot these messages and forward them to Tyler. He needs to know."

I wince. "There's nothing he can do about them tonight. And if I tell him, he might go after Brad and possibly end up in jail again."

"You can't keep this from him," Liam says.

"I won't. I'll tell Tyler tomorrow, I swear. After the ceremony, when we're on our way to Key West, and he can't do anything crazy."

Liam frowns. "You'd better."

"I will. I promise."

By the time the movie ends, we're all nicely buzzed. We end up watching another one—a Marvel superhero movie this time, not another horror flick. I've had enough of blood and gore for one night. Liam hands out pints of ice cream and brownies so we can binge on sugar.

A little after midnight, we all crash on the living room floor in sleeping bags. "Thanks, guys," I say as Liam turns off the lights. "This was a lot of fun." I roll onto my side and hug my pillow, wishing it were Tyler.

๑ 18

Tyler Jamison

I t's a beautiful autumn day, perfect for a wedding. The air is crisp and fresh, and the colorful leaves haven't all fallen yet.

Shane and Beth's estate is filled to the brim with people—my family, Ian's family, and the entire McIntyre clan. Gina Capelli and her small catering staff are here setting up for the reception after the ceremony. The florists have already come and gone. The photographer is wandering around taking pictures of everyone. Jonah

Locke, Lia McIntyre's rockstar husband, is playing an acoustic guitar in the great room. Even Jud Walker, my former boss and my father's best friend, is here. Jud has been a surrogate father to me since my dad died. There were tears in his eyes when he hugged me.

I'm overwhelmed that all these people are here for my wedding—for *our* wedding.

According to my spies—Liam and Sam—Ian is currently holed up in our suite on the second floor, being coddled as he prepares for the ceremony. From what I hear, he has no shortage of help from Beth and our mother, and from Layla and their mother. I still haven't seen what he's planning to wear during the ceremony. I did get a quick glimpse at what was in his garment bag, and I saw a whole lot of white. It seems fitting that I'm wearing black, and he's wearing white. After all, he is the light to my darkness.

I'm waiting with Cooper and Shane in the library, which is right off the foyer. We're ready to go, just waiting for our cue.

"You nervous?" Cooper asks. He looks impressive in a black suit and tie. It's rare that I see him in anything other than plaid flannel and blue jeans.

Checking my reflection in a mirror, I adjust my tie for

the umpteenth time. "No. Today is just a formality. You say a few words, we say *I do*, and it's done."

Shane laughs. "You're not fooling anyone, detective."

I roll my eyes at him. "I'm no longer a detective."

"You're a private investigator," Cooper notes. "That's still a detective of sorts."

"Good point," Shane says. He claps me on the shoulder. "So, the name sticks."

Cooper adjusts the boutonniere pinned to my breast pocket. "You look good, man. I'll give you that."

Before I can reply, there's a brisk knock at the door. Then a deep male voice says, "Twenty minutes to show time, fellas."

"That's Jake," Shane says, naming one of his many brothers.

Shane pulls on his black tux jacket and straightens his tie. "I'm ready."

"Me, too," Cooper says.

I turn to face them. "Thank you both for your support today. It means a lot to me. I know I haven't always been your favorite person."

Shane laughs. "That's an understatement." He pats my back. "But don't worry. You've grown on us."

Finally, it's time for us to take our places. We leave the

library and pause outside the great room, which is divided in half by a center aisle, with rows of folding chairs lined up on both sides. Courtesy of the florist, the room is decorated with fresh greenery and bouquets of teal calla lilies and cream-colored roses. Seeing all that teal makes me smile.

Cooper enters first. "We're ready to get started, folks, so take your seats."

The few people who are standing around chatting sit. Jonah continues playing classical music on his acoustic guitar.

When he reaches his destination at the front of the room, Cooper turns to face the guests. He motions for me and Shane to come forward, and we walk down the aisle, first me, then Shane.

The room hushes, and we hear only a quiet murmur of voices.

Just before I reach the front of the room, I pause to acknowledge my mom, who's seated in the front row, to my right. She holds out her hand, and I take it, giving it a gentle squeeze. Her eyes are glistening with tears, and she's doing her best to keep it together. Jud is seated beside her.

I lean down and kiss my mother's soft cheek. "I bet

you thought this day would never come."

She smiles up at me. "I'm so happy for you, darling," she whispers. She touches my cheek. "You deserve to be happy."

Jud shakes my hand. "Your father would be so proud right now."

I move forward to stand beside Cooper. Shane's right behind me, stopping a moment to squeeze my mom's hand and shake Jud's.

While we wait for the rest of the wedding party to make their entrance, my mind races as I scan the small crowd gathered here. All of these people are here for us. When my sister married into the McIntyre family, I gained more family and friends than I could ever imagine.

ℰ 19

Ian Alexander

I stare at my reflection in a full-length mirror and marvel at how I came to be in this place, in this very moment, about to marry the man of my dreams. Tyler's my hero—literally. He saved me from Roy Valdez, who attempted to kill me. He also saved me metaphorically by offering me unconditional love and a soul-deep connection I never thought I would find.

Beth, my soon-to-be sister-in-law, comes up beside me and smiles as she slips her arm around my waist. She meets my gaze in the mirror. "You look amazing, Ian."

I laugh shakily. "You're just being nice. Tyler's the one who is swoonworthy." I'm just... me. The white tuxedo jacket fits me beautifully. The matching slacks fit me just the way I like, hugging my ass. My hair is curling perfectly on top, and my undercut is freshly trimmed. I am *so* ready.

I slip my arm around Beth and hug her back. She looks divine in a pale aqua silk dress that matches her blue-green eyes—the same unusual color eyes as Tyler's. Her long blonde hair is swept up in an intricate topknot, a few curling tendrils hanging down. There's a slender gold chain around her neck that holds a locket containing pictures of her husband and kids. I'm not just gaining a husband. I'm expanding my family to include Tyler's family as well.

Today has to be the best day of my life.

Layla walks up on my other side, a big smile on her face. She's wearing a burgundy sheath dress and contrasts beautifully with her black hair. "Tyler's going to die when he sees you." She straightens my bow tie, which coordinates perfectly with the calla lilies in my boutonniere.

"I hope you mean that figuratively," I say as I pull my

sister close.

My mom joins us. Her dark, auburn hair is up in a sleek bun. She looks elegant in a silky, embroidered teal dress she chose specifically because it matches my tie. "I think you're ready," she says, smiling brightly. She's doing her best to pretend her eyes aren't tearing up already.

"Mom, please don't cry, or you'll make me cry." I glance around the room looking for a clock. "What time is it? I don't want to be late to my own wedding."

"Relax, honey," Mom says as she pats my arm. "We have ten minutes."

The ceremony is scheduled to start at two.

There's a knock on the door, and a female voice says, "Ian, it's almost time. You should head downstairs now."

"That's Sophie," Beth says.

Shane's eldest sister, Sophie—formerly a McIntyre, but now Sophie Zaretti after her marriage to Dominic—has been acting as our social director since we arrived. She's been keeping us all on schedule. Despite being pregnant, nothing slows Sophie down. She's in her element here. And the rest of us are getting a kick out of watching her beast of a husband, Dominic, dog her every step to make sure she doesn't overdo it.

"Ian?" Sophie knocks once more and speaks through

the closed door. "May I have your wedding band, please? We need it for the ring bearer pillow."

"All right, but you better not lose it." Reluctantly, I slip my ring off my finger. Beth takes it from me, cracks open the door, and hands it to Sophie.

"Don't worry, Ian," Sophie says through the door. "You'll get it back in no time."

"All right, let's go downstairs." Beth opens the door. "Let's go meet up with Aiden and Luke in the foyer."

Aiden McIntyre, Jake's adopted six-year-old son, will carry our wedding bands to Tyler on a small white silk pillow. Luke is our flower boy—I'm not sure how that's going to go. We would have included Aiden's twin sisters in the wedding party, too, but they're way too young.

I slip my feet into my newly polished black Oxfords and follow the girls downstairs to the foyer. Muffled voices drift out of the great room, along with quiet guitar music, courtesy of Jonah.

I seriously can't believe Jonah Locke is playing at my wedding. What's even more amazing is that he's going to sing covers of some of my favorite songs when it comes time for the dancing. Social media would go crazy if folks knew he was here. Maybe I can sneak some pics of him to post online.

My groomsmen are already lined up outside the great room and ready to make their entrance. They all look dashingly handsome in their black tuxes.

Standing beside my friends are Aiden and Luke. Aiden's mother, Annie, is straightening his little bow tie, which matches mine. Luke is currently in the arms of his paternal grandma, Bridget McIntyre, his blond head resting on her shoulder as he sucks his thumb. The little guy is tired—probably because he missed his morning nap.

Beth props open the double doors leading into the great room, and I gasp when I spot Tyler standing across the room next to Cooper and Shane. I snag Beth's hand and squeeze it hard. "Oh, my god. Your brother looks magnificent."

She chuckles. "So do you." She rises up on her tippy toes to kiss my cheek. "I couldn't wish for a better partner for my brother."

When Jonah starts strumming *Pachelbel's Canon in D Major*, Cooper signals us to start the procession.

Bridget sets Luke on his feet and turns him to face the great room. The boy's paternal grandfather, Calum, hands the toddler a white wicker basket filled with cream-colored rose petals.

Bridget crouches down beside Luke and points straight down the aisle at Shane, who's standing beside Tyler. "There's Daddy, Luke. Go to Daddy."

Looking more than a bit confused, Luke takes a few steps forward, but then he stops, glances around uncertainly, and turns to run back to Beth.

"Throw the flowers, honey," Beth says. "Just like we practiced, remember? Throw the flowers on the floor and go to Daddy."

Luke grabs a handful of rose petals and tosses them straight up into the air, pausing to watch as they drift to the floor at his feet. When a few petals land softly on his head, he brushes them off. The resulting quiet laughter from the attendees encourages him to do it again.

Grinning, Shane crouches down in front of the assembled guests and holds out his arms. "Come here, Luke." He waves the boy forward. "Come here, buddy. Come to Daddy."

Suddenly having lost interest in the rose petals, Luke drops the basket on the floor and runs to his father. Shane scoops him up and kisses his cheek. "Good boy. Close enough."

The guests are laughing as Shane hands his son off to his mother, who's now seated in the front row on the left side of the room, next to his father.

"It's my turn now, isn't it?" Aiden asks. He gazes up at me with big brown puppy dog eyes.

Liam ruffles the kid's brown hair. "You're on, kid. Go for it."

Taking his role very seriously, Aiden walks sedately down the aisle and stands beside Tyler and Shane, clutching the pillow tightly in his little hands.

The groomsmen are next—Liam, Miguel, Sam, Philip, Chris, and Trey—and they walk toward the front of the room.

Finally, it's my turn. When Jonah switches to a lovely instrumental version of *I Can't Help Falling In Love With You*, Cooper waves me forward.

My parents join me, one on each side, and we link arms. They walk me down the aisle toward my waiting groom. The entire time, my gaze is glued to Tyler's, and his is locked onto mine. He doesn't take his eyes off me, not for a second.

This is it.

It's really happening.

When we reach Tyler, my parents hand me over to my husband-to-be. As I stand before him, my pulse races, and I feel lightheaded.

Tyler squeezes my hand and smiles. "Breathe, baby, before you pass out." Then he leans close and whispers, "You look absolutely amazing."

⎛⎠ 20

Tyler Jamison

As Ian approaches the altar, I realize I've been holding my breath in anticipation of seeing him. Finally, I get to see what all the fuss is about. He's wearing a white tux with a white shirt and a pale teal bow tie. He looks utterly amazing. I can't take my eyes off him. He's watching me so intently, my throat tightens, and my vision blurs. When I wipe a tear from my cheek, Shane lays a supportive hand on my back.

Ian's parents walk him down the aisle, their arms

linked with his. It's obvious Ruth has been crying. But even though her eyes are rimmed with red, she's beaming with pride. She looks lovely in a full-length teal dress. Martin looks debonaire in a black tux. His teal cummerbund matches his wife's dress.

As Ian nears, we only have eyes for each other. The rest of the room fades into the background.

I think back to the years—to the *decades*—of loneliness I experienced before meeting Ian. All the times I tried—and failed—to connect with women. Growing up, I thought something was wrong with me. I didn't understand why I couldn't be happy. I never dreamed I was looking in the wrong place.

It wasn't until I crossed paths with a charismatic young man in the back hallway of a bar that I finally felt a spark of attraction. I remember clearly how he looked at me, fearless and so confident. It was as if he knew me better than I knew myself.

I was lost the moment I laid eyes on him.

And now I'm marrying the man of my dreams.

When Ian finally reaches my side, his parents graciously hand him over to me, placing his hand in mine, as if symbolically they're placing him in my safekeeping. I want to assure them that no matter what comes our way, I will protect their son with my life. I'll do my best to make him happy and provide him with everything he needs.

As Cooper begins speaking, Ian and I turn to face each other. I reach for his other hand, and he clutches mine fervently.

Finally, when it's my turn to repeat my vows, my voice shakes. "I, Tyler Jamison, take thee, Ian Alexander, to be my lawfully wedded husband, to have and to hold from this day forward, for better or worse, for richer or poorer, in sickness and in health, to love and to cherish, 'til death do us part."

Then it's Ian's turn. His eyes are wide and glistening with unshed tears as he recites his vows. "I, Ian Alexander, take thee, Tyler Jamison, to be my lawfully wedded husband...."

When Ian has recited his vows, Cooper smiles down at Aiden, who's standing still as a statue beside me. "We're ready for the rings, son."

With all the seriousness a six-year-old can muster, Aiden holds the pillow up to me. I loosen the ribbon holding our wedding bands. I slip Ian's band onto his ring finger, and he does the same for me.

Cooper's deep voice is loud and clear when he finally

declares, "I now pronounce you husband and husband."

Our families and friends cheer.

Cooper winks at me. "That's your cue to kiss him."

I cup Ian's face in my hands and kiss him in front of everyone, amidst cheers and applause and a few hoots and hollers.

After our kiss, we turn to face everyone. I raise our clasped hands high in the air, feeling a sense of triumph I've never experienced in my life.

We did it.

He's mine.

Now and forever.

After that moment, chaos ensues. Our parents and sisters rush forward to hug us. There's lots of laughter and kissing. Somehow, miraculously, the chairs are pushed to the perimeter, opening up space in the center of the room.

My sister slips her arm around my waist and pulls me close to whisper, "It's time for your first dance as a married couple."

Oh, god. The part I've been dreading.

My heart hammers in my chest as blood rushes to my head. Dancing in front of a crowd is way out of my comfort zone. But it's for Ian's sake. Today is his wedding day, and I don't want to disappoint him. If he asked me to, I'd dance on the tabletops.

I turn to my new husband and offer him my arm. "May I have the honor of this dance?"

Ian's eyes widen in genuine surprise. "Really? You'll dance with me?"

"Of course I will."

He grins as he links his elbow with mine. "I would love to."

As I lead Ian to the center of the dance floor, a hush falls over the room as everyone gathers around us. I do my best to focus on Ian's beaming face and block out the curious onlookers.

This is for Ian.

Jonah starts strumming the opening chords to one of Ian's favorite songs, *You Are the Reason* by Calum Scott. As soon as the I hear the familiar melody, a sense of calm comes over me.

As we take our first steps in a slow waltz of sorts, Ian gazes at me with real concern etching his features. "Are you sure you're okay with this? We don't have to dance. It's enough that you offered."

"I'm sure."

He smiles at me through tear-filled eyes, his expression broadcasting his amazement.

"I would do anything for you, Ian." It's the truth. He's the reason I can't wait to go to bed every night, and he's the first thought in my head every morning when I wake up. He makes *everything* better.

I tighten my hold on him, drawing him closer, and he glides effortlessly in step with me. It's not that I don't know how to dance. My mother made sure of it when I was a teenager in case I ever went to a school dance— which I never did. Still, the lessons have come in handy today. I just don't like being the center of attention.

With each step, I feel myself relaxing in Ian's arms. He's looking at me like I just hung the moon for him. It's easy to forget about everything else.

Before I know it, the song ends and another one begins. I'm not in any hurry to stop dancing with my husband, so we continue without missing a beat as Jonah sings another one of Ian's favorite songs. "Did you give Jonah a song list?"

Ian grins sheepishly. "Maybe."

I break our gaze for a moment to scan the crowd. I'm looking for my mother, and when I spot her standing near the front of the crowd, she's beaming at us. Beth has her arm around Mom's waist, and they're watching us intently.

Ian surprises me by leading me across the floor. He takes Mom's hand and lays it in mine. "Ingrid, dance with your very handsome son."

Mom steps forward, smiling through her tears.

"Hi, Mom," I say as I pull her into my arms.

"You look so much like your father. I wish he could be here today. He'd be so proud of you."

My chest tightens at the mention of my father. His absence is an eternal hole in my heart. "I like to think he would have approved."

She nods. "I know he would have. He loved you so much."

It's then that I notice Ian dancing with his mother. And suddenly, we're joined on the dance floor by a third couple when Sam drags Cooper out onto the dance floor and sweeps him into his arms. Our onlookers cheer.

Cooper is just as uncomfortable in front of a crowd as I am, so I know this isn't easy for him. I catch his gaze and nod. He gives me a bashful smile and shrugs.

Soon, other couples join us on the floor. Beth and Shane. Layla and Jason. Shane's parents. Most of Shane's siblings and their spouses or partners join the dancing. Martin steals Ruth away from Ian, and Joe Rucker steals my mom from me.

Finally, Ian and I are back in each other's arms just as Jonah segues to a new song, *A Thousand Years* by Christina Perri. Ian beams when he hears the song. I don't think I've ever seen him so happy.

"Hello, Mr. Jamison," I tell him.

"Hello to you, too, Mr. Jamison." Then he leans in and kisses me.

Before the song is even over, our sisters descend on us. Beth steals Ian for a dance, and Layla claims me.

"I'm so happy for you both, I could scream," Layla says as she gazes up at me.

"Please don't. We don't want to give poor Jason a heart attack."

She laughs.

On reflex, we both glance across the room to see Jason standing with Liam and Miguel. Even though the three of them are deep in conversation, Jason's got one eye on Layla. I doubt she's ever out of his sight. He takes his responsibility as her bodyguard very seriously, and being her boyfriend only intensifies his need to protect her.

Layla squeezes my hand. "I'm so happy for you both. You two were made for each other." Her smile turns sad. "I'll never forget what you did for me, Tyler. You saved my life, despite what it cost you."

I glance down just as her dark eyes tear up. "I would do it all over again in a heartbeat."

✒ 21

Ian Jamison

Mind if I break up this love fest so I can dance with my best girl?" Cooper asks as he steals Beth from me.

She laughs as he whisks her away.

Since he's practically her adopted father, I'll let him get away with it.

Grinning, Sam pulls me into his arms. "Sorry, but it looks like you're stuck with me. So, how does it feel to be a married man?"

"It feels freaking fantastic."

"I'll bet it does." Sam glances across the dance floor at his partner, who's dipping a laughing Beth over his arm.

"I can't wait to see you and Cooper tie the knot." When Sam's cheeks redden, I say, "Oh, my god, you're blushing."

"Hopefully one of these days," Sam says. "You have no idea what it's taken for me to get Cooper this far. When we first met, he was so deep in the closet he couldn't see daylight. He was all about nameless one-night stands, with absolutely zero interest in dating, let alone having a serious relationship. He's mine now, and that's what matters. We'll tie the knot when he's ready. I'll wait." Sam tips his head to his left. "Adorableness at nine o'clock."

I turn to see what he's looking at. One of Shane's brothers, Jake, is dancing with his wife, Annie. They're each holding one of their twin baby girls. Annie says something that makes Jake laugh. He leans in and kisses his wife.

Sam spins me in a circle. "You and Tyler would be great parents."

"That would be a dream come true. Can you imagine Tyler as a father?" I shiver. "Damn."

When the current song ends, Sophie calls Tyler and

me over to the cake table. Our wedding cake is gorgeous. Three tiers of almond vanilla pound cake covered in sleek white marzipan icing, decorated with pale teal roses and tiny, edible gold beads. The cake topper is the best part, though. Gina had two custom figurines made that resemble us perfectly.

There's lots of love and laughter all around us, but I only have eyes for my new husband. He's so handsome he makes my heart flutter and my pulse race. I feel positively giddy.

Sophie hands Tyler a long, serrated knife. "Here you go, Tyler. You get to cut the first slice."

He cuts the first slice of cake, picks it up with his fingers, and brings it to my mouth.

As soon as that vanilla flavor hits my tongue, I groan. "Oh, wow, that's good. Where's Gina?" I scan the crowd for Gina, spotting her standing next to her brother, Peter. "Gina, you outdid yourself, sweetie. This cake is divine."

She smiles. "I'm so glad you like it, Ian."

Now it's my turn to cut a piece for Tyler. He hands me the knife—hilt first, of course. *He's such a Boy Scout.* He gives me a silent, pleading look that says, *Please don't shove cake in my face.*

Like a good husband, I cut a piece for him and carefully bring it to his mouth. As he takes a cautious bite, his gaze locks onto mine, and it's like we're the only ones in the room. There's so much heat in his eyes. His look of utter satisfaction sinks deep into my soul. "You're enjoying this, aren't you?" I ask.

Tyler nods. "Of course, I am. I'm sharing wedding cake with my husband. What could be better?"

Heat rises in my cheeks. "Well... I can think of a few things."

He leans in close enough that his lips graze my ear. "How soon can we leave?" His warm breath glazes my skin, making me shiver. Naturally, he notices. Tyler never misses a thing. "You'll do a lot more than shiver tonight, baby. Trust me."

Now I'm blushing. "You are such a bad man."

He laughs. "You have no idea."

After everyone has cake, Sophie pulls me to the front of the room and makes an announcement. "All right, all you single ladies. Gather round. Ian's going to toss his boutonniere."

There are lots of chuckles in the room as family members herd the single women to the front of the crowd. Sophie turns me so that my back is to the women. She removes my boutonniere and hands it to me. "All right,

Ian. Toss it over your shoulder. Whoever catches it will be the next one to get married."

I fling the boutonniere behind me, and when I hear boisterous cheers, I turn to see Molly Ferguson, Jamie McIntyre's girlfriend, holding it cradled in her hands. She blushes as Jamie wraps her in his arms.

We move on to the photography. We hired a wedding photographer to videotape the ceremony and the reception. She then takes pictures of all the family, the guests, and of course the wedding party.

While I'm watching the photographer take photos of Tyler and his family, Annie and Sophie join me.

"Congratulations, Ian," Annie says as she hugs me with one arm. She's holding one of her baby girls in her other arm. The dark-haired little beauties are truly identical. Pretty much only Annie and her son, Aiden, can tell them apart. I hear that even Jake struggles to keep the girls straight.

I hug her back. "Thank you. Which baby is this?"

"Everly," she says, grinning as she gazes at her dark-eyed little princess. "Jake has Emerly." Across the room, as Jake helps Cooper man the bar, he has the other twin propped on his hip.

"I hear you two are heading to Key West tonight," Sophie says.

I nod. "Our flight leaves at eight."

She sighs. "I'm so envious. The days are getting cooler and shorter here far too quickly for my taste. I'm jealous that you'll be living it up in sunshine and hot temperatures."

"That's the plan," Tyler says as he comes up behind me. He slips his arm around my waist. "By the way, you're needed." He nods toward the photographer. "She's taking pictures of your family now."

Everly reaches for Tyler's boutonniere, but he catches her hand. "Careful, sweetheart," he says as he gently redirects her attention. "It's got a pin in it. Owie."

Of course he'd make a wonderful father, I tell myself as I join my family on the back deck, which overlooks Lake Michigan. It's the perfect backdrop for our wedding photos.

* * *

After all the festivities are over and everyone is heading home, Tyler and I head straight for the airport to catch our flight. Our bags are already packed and stored in the trunk of Tyler's car. Jerry offered to drive us so we don't have to leave the car parked at the airport all week.

This late in the evening, the airport lines aren't as long as usual. We check our bags, including Tyler's locked gun case. Thanks to his career in law enforcement, Tyler already has a license to carry in Florida.

We wait in line with our carry-on bags to pass through security checkpoint. Before we know it, we're at our departure gate waiting to be seated on board our flight.

After we're seated, I glance around. I know there's a bar around here somewhere. I check the time. "We have at least forty-five minutes to kill before our flight boards. Why don't we have a celebratory drink?"

Tyler grins. "I have a feeling we'll be doing a lot of celebrating this week."

"Of course we will! We're married." I'm dying to reach for his hand, but we're in public, and I don't want to make him feel self-conscious. Being in a same-sex relationship is still kind of new for him. I wonder how he'll do when we get to our destination. We're booked at a men-only, LGBTQ-friendly resort, so we won't be getting a lot of unwelcome stares. I want him to be able to relax and enjoy his honeymoon.

Tyler nods toward the bar. "Let's go."

"Yay!" I jump to my feet and start walking. He's right

behind me.

The bar is small, dark, and intimate. I find a private table for two in the back.

"What can I get you?" asks the young woman who comes to take our order.

"Whiskey," Tyler says.

I refrain from rolling my eyes. "Seriously? You have absolutely no imagination." To our server, I say, "I'll have a Unicorn Shot, please. Extra whipped cream and sprinkles."

She looks at me like I'm speaking a foreign language. "Um, I'm not sure we make those. I'll have to ask the bartender."

I smile. "You do that, thanks, sweetie."

After she walks away, Tyler gives me a droll look. "Are you trying to cause trouble?"

"No. I'm on my honeymoon, and I want to have fun." I reach for his hand.

To my surprise, he gives it to me. "And I want you to have all the fun you can stand."

When our server returns, she sets Tyler's whiskey in front of him. Then she sets my gorgeous Unicorn shot on the table. It looks amazing, bright pink liquor topped with whipped cream and pastel heart-shaped sprinkles.

Tyler looks absolutely horrified. "What in the hell is that?"

"Strawberry vodka, white chocolate liqueur, strawberry liqueur, strawberry milk, whipped cream, blue frosting, mini marshmallows, and of course sprinkles."

"So, basically it's a grown-up version of strawberry milk."

"Pretty much. Do you want to try it?" I taste it before sliding the glass to him.

He picks it up and takes a sip, leaving a bit of whipped cream and some of the blue frosting on his mustache. "It's not horrible."

I point to his upper lip. "You have a little something there."

His tongue swipes across his lip, and the whipped cream disappears. *Damn.* That certainly gives me ideas.

Tyler passes my drink back to me. "I think I'll stick with whiskey."

I make a face. "Whiskey is going to taste really nasty after that."

He laughs. "I imagine you're right." He sips his whiskey and tries valiantly not to make a face, but he fails.

I laugh, not just because he's being a good sport by stepping outside his comfort zone, but because I'm excited to be getting out of town with him. We're heading to Key West, the land of sun and fun. It's going to be amazing. I reach for his hand again. "I want us to go on moonlit strolls along the beach. I want to snorkel and sail with you. I want to go to bars and eat incredible food and drink rainbow cocktails."

His thumb strokes the back of my hand. "I'm looking forward to it."

I take another sip of my delicious cocktail. "I wish we were there already."

He looks at his watch. "It won't be long now."

ᐢ 22

Tyler Jamison

Our flight to Key West International Airport is uneventful. Ian has a window seat, and his eyes are glued to the wide expanse of blue-green water that stretches as far as the eye can see. He keeps patting my leg to get my attention. "Look at that water. Tell me again why we live in Chicago. We should live here. Should we buy a place? Maybe a whole island."

"Are you serious?" But of course he is. He can certainly afford to buy an island.

He shrugs. "Sure. Why not?"

As we make our final approach, Ian turns to me, his eyes alight with anticipation. "We're here."

As soon as we step outside of the airport, we're greeted by warm, humid air—a welcome change from the chilly temperatures back home.

Ian spreads his arms wide and turns in a circle, a big smile on his face. "Oh, my god, this heat feels so good. This is exactly what I needed."

We pick up our car—a bright blue Corvette convertible that Ian arranged through a private rental agency—and load our luggage into the trunk. I don't even want to know what it cost to rent a car this flashy for a whole week.

We drive down the coast to the resort. Our hotel is located right on the ocean, with direct access to a private beach. Even though it's well after dark when we arrive, a hotel attendant is standing by to welcome us.

"Misters Jamison," he says with a polished smile. "Welcome! The Presidential Honeymoon Suite is ready for you." He starts loading our luggage onto a rolling cart.

An eager young valet steps forward and hands Ian a ticket. Ian hands him the key.

Despite the late hour, guests are strolling in and

out of the resort's front doors. Ian booked our stay at a men-only resort. And according to a sign out front, clothing is optional. Although, looking around, I see everyone is dressed to some extent, even if only in skimpy swim trunks. I did not bring a pair of Speedos, although Ian did.

I gaze up at the front façade of this five-star hotel surrounded by towering palm trees and observe the couples streaming in and out of the hotel. The men are mostly couples holding hands, laughing, and teasing. I see lots of brightly-colored clothing and carefree smiles. I'm dressed in black jeans and a gray short-sleeve button-down. "I stick out like a sore thumb."

Ian laughs. "You're fine." He grabs my hand and leans close to whisper, "You don't have to be fabulous to be gay. There are lots of gay men who feel more at home in flannel shirts and blue jeans. There's no one-size-fits-all. You do you, babe."

I gaze down at my attire. "I'm hardly a lumberjack."

"Right. That would be Cooper. You're my perfect match."

"Which is?"

He pauses to think a moment. "Let's see—grumpy, controlling, domineering—" His eyes light up at that last adjective. "Definitely my type."

"Okay, I get the picture." I motion for Ian to proceed me into the hotel. "Let's get checked in."

After we sign in at the front desk and receive our key cards, we take the elevator to the top floor. As we approach the honeymoon suite, I sweep Ian off his feet and into my arms.

Ian gasps as he throws his arms around my neck. "Oh, my god," he says, laughing. "Can you be any sexier?"

I smile as I carry him to our door. He pulls out his key-card, swipes the lock, and turns the doorknob. I push the door open with my shoulder and carry him inside. "I'm supposed to carry you over the threshold, right?"

We step inside a spacious, beautifully decorated suite that includes vaulted ceilings, a living room with a gas fireplace and the biggest TV I've ever seen, an eat-in gourmet kitchen, a bedroom with a king-size bed, and a bathroom with an impressive Jacuzzi.

We find our luggage sitting neatly on the floor at the foot of the bed. Ian walks over to the bedroom balcony doors and throws open the drapes, revealing an ocean view—I'm sure we're paying a pretty penny for the privilege.

"Oh, my god, look at that," he says.

I join him at the glass doors just as he opens them and steps out onto our private balcony. I follow him out. It is a beautiful view, I must admit. The ocean is straight ahead, like something from a postcard. It's a clear night, and the stars are out in force. Moonlight shines down on the rippling water. Even from here, we can hear the sound of the waves lapping on the beach.

Ian turns to me and grasps the front of my T-shirt. "We're going to have so much fun. No work. No responsibilities. Just fun and relaxation." He runs his hand down the front of my shirt. "And lots of kissing and cuddling and sexy times." He kisses me.

I grasp Ian's hips and draw him close. "What would you like to do first, Mr. Jamison?"

Ian grins. "I want to celebrate with my husband." He pulls me back into the bedroom, where we find an ice bucket sitting on a round table just inside the balcony doors. There's a bottle of champagne wedged into the ice and two flutes on the table. A little gift box sitting on the tabletop contains variety of chocolate truffles from a local candy shop.

"They've thought of everything," Ian says as he wanders over to the bed.

The white bed cover is littered with red rose petals.

There are two decorative pillows each monogrammed with *Mr.* All throughout the room are battery-operated candles that flicker like the real thing.

Ian gazes at our luggage. "That can wait until morning. This can't." And he takes my hands in his and faces me, his expression so earnest. My breath catches in my throat as he gazes at me with so much love. It's both humbling and mind-blowing to me that this gorgeous, charismatic man wants me.

"I can't believe we're married," he says.

I pull him into my arms, my hand cupping the back of his head as I stare into his eyes. "Thank you, Ian, for saving me from myself. For giving me a life filled with joy and purpose."

He swallows hard. "Babe, you already had those things."

I don't think he can ever truly understand how lonely I was before I met him. Instead, I walk over to the ice bucket, grab the bottle of champagne, and pop off the top. I pour us each a glass and hand him one. "To us. To a long, happy life."

"Here's to growing old together." Ian takes a sip.

"I think I saw a Jacuzzi in the bathroom. Shall we?" I set down my glass, pull off my shirt, and toss it onto the bed.

Smiling, Ian follows my lead and begins undressing.

I fill the tub while Ian dims the lights. He retrieves the champagne bottle and our glasses so we can continue enjoying what I'm sure is a very expensive bottle of bubbly.

The hot water feels like heaven. I lean back in the tub, and Ian sits between my legs and relaxes back against my chest.

"I meant every word I said today," I tell him as I wrap my arms around him and hold him close. "For better and for worse, until death do us part. I will honor our vows—I will honor *you*—the very best that I can. I will try to be the husband you deserve. I want to make you happy, Ian. Not just content, but truly happy."

"You've already succeeded. I can't imagine being happier than I am right now." He turns to press his lips to mine.

"So, what's on the agenda for tomorrow?" I ask.

"Plenty. We should go for a long walk on the beach, swim in the ocean, walk into town and eat amazing food at fantastic restaurants. And we need to go shopping for souvenirs. Tomorrow evening, I'll take you to The Pink Triangle—it's a section of Duval Street that's home to a number of LGBTQ-friendly bars and nightclubs."

I laugh. "Ian, we're going to be here for an entire week. We don't have to do it all in one day."

"Hey, that's not all. We should also charter a boat and take a private cruise around the island. We should go snorkeling and swim with dolphins." He sighs. "The list is endless."

I wrap my arms around his waist and kiss the side of his neck, smiling when he shivers. My lips trail across his firm shoulder. "You're going to wear me out this week."

He laughs. "Baby, I'm going to wear you out *tonight*."

My hands start wandering as I caress his chest, pausing to tease his nipples. I slide my fingers down the front of his torso, over his belly, to his hips. He groans when I wrap my fingers around his length and start leisurely stroking him. Immediately, he hardens. I slide my fist up his entire length and down, again and again, slowly, making sure he feels every inch of my touch, trying to draw out every bit of pleasure.

His breaths come faster now. With a groan, Ian rests his head back on my shoulder and grips my thighs.

I take my time stroking him, letting my fingers graze his entire length. "Shall we go see if that bed is as comfortable as it looks?"

"Oh, god, yes. You go relax. I'll join you in a little bit."

We brush our teeth at the bathroom vanity, with his and his sinks. While I pull back the bed coverings, Ian grabs his toiletries bag and disappears back into the bathroom.

I turn down the bedroom lights and open the drapes to let the warm sea breeze in. I can still hear the muted voices of guests relaxing in the pool below our balcony.

While I'm waiting for Ian, I unpack our suitcases, hang up our clothing and stow the rest of our clothes in the dresser drawers. I put a few necessary items from my toiletries bag in the top drawer of my nightstand for easy reach. My locked gun case goes in the safe located in the bedroom closet.

The room is beautifully romantic, with the lights down low and fake candles flickering all around the room, on the dresser, on the nightstands. A row of them line the wood mantle above the gas fireplace. Everything's perfect.

Just as I strip off my shirt and lay it aside, I hear a sound behind me. I turn to find Ian standing in the open bathroom doorway, naked and fully erect.

My gaze skims him from head to toe, taking note of the set of his shoulders, the breadth of his chest, his pecs and abs. My gaze follows the narrowing line of hair that leads down to his groin.

The sight of him takes my breath away.

I cross the room to stand before him and cup his face. "You're beautiful." I lean in to kiss him. He smells like warm man and soap, and he tastes like peppermint.

Laying his palms on my bare chest, Ian smiles. "It's our honeymoon. Our first time together as husbands."

My heart thuds in my chest. This is a momentous occasion. It's not like we haven't been together before, many times. But tonight, this means something special.

Our honeymoon.

I take Ian's hands in mine and walk backward toward the bed. When the back of my knees hit the mattress, I sit on the edge of the bed and pull Ian close. I wrap my fingers around his length and hold him firmly.

His chest rises as he sucks in a strong breath.

With my free hand, I reach around to caress his buttock, stroking and squeezing his flesh. I run my fingertip along the crease between those round cheeks, watching Ian's expression to gauge his arousal.

His nostrils flare as his breathing picks up.

I open my mouth and swallow his cock deep, until he's nearly at the back of my throat. He's throbbing already, thick and flushed with heat. While my tongue and lips worship him, my fingers knead his ass cheeks, squeezing and molding his flesh. I tease his opening, smiling as he clenches and releases his muscles.

Ian's hands grasp my head, clutching at me as he starts to move, thrusting into my mouth. I pull back, releasing him. "Not yet, baby. There's so much more to come tonight."

I stand to shuck off my PJ bottoms and nod to the bed, and while he climbs onto the mattress, I open the nightstand top drawer and remove a bottle of lube, leaving it within easy reach.

As I lie back, I draw Ian over me so that he's straddling my lap. He aligns his erection with mine and takes us both in his hand and starts stroking. I watch him handle us both in his firm grip. The heads of our cocks brush together in a perfect choreography of motion.

Both of us are breathing hard now, our chests heaving.

He strokes us until we're both nearly on the edge, flushed and throbbing, so close to coming.

I gently remove his hand, grab the bottle of lube, and dribble some along my length, coating myself.

Ian rises up on his knees and reaches back to position me so that he can sink down on me until he's fully sheathed. Then he starts moving, with my help. He raises himself and sinks down on me.

I sit up and hold him to me, then roll us so that he's on his back. I kneel between his thighs and sink all the way in. His hands go to my torso, and he strokes my chest, my shoulders and arms.

I move slowly and steadily, never once taking my gaze from his. So much emotion and feeling passes between us without a single word being spoken. I lean down and kiss him, then trail my lips down his throat to his chest. I tease his nipples, licking and flicking them with my tongue.

Ian takes hold of his cock and strokes himself vigorously, and I speed my thrusts to match his.

He comes first, with a gasp and a cry. I follow right behind him, a deep groan rising from my throat. My chest heaves as I try to catch my breath.

After I withdraw, I sink down beside him on the mattress and pull him in my arms. We lie there and hold each other for a while, until the sweat on our skin dries and we feel the cooling night air.

I grab a wet washcloth from the bathroom and clean us up. Then I join Ian in bed, and we snuggle.

"I love you, Mr. Jamison," I say as I stroke his back.

Ian tightens his arms around me. "I love you, too, Mr. Jamison."

23

Ian Jamison

The moment my brain comes online in the morning, the first thing that registers is Tyler's warm body pressed against my back. He's the big spoon, always. I'm the little spoon. I stretch, groaning loudly.

Tyler tightens his arm around my waist. "Don't move," he growls. He almost sounds hungover, but I know that's not possible. We only had a little champagne last night.

I do move. In fact, I wiggle my ass against his groin

and smile when I feel an erection prodding my backside. "Why not?"

He groans. "Because this feels too good."

I press back even harder against him. "I know what would feel even better."

That earns me a light slap on my hip. "I'll be right back." He gets up and heads to the bathroom. I hear the toilet flush and water running in the sink. A few moments later, he's back and crawling into bed.

I follow his lead and head to the john myself to pee and freshen up.

When I rejoin him in bed, he presses his lips to the back of my neck. Then he rolls me onto my back. "Last night was our first night together as a married couple."

I thread my fingers through his messy dark hair. "Yeah?" I'm curious where this is going.

"This morning is our first morning together as a married couple. What would you like to do?"

"How about breakfast? I saw a sign last night in the hotel lobby advertising an all-you-can-eat breakfast buffet from seven until ten."

He checks the time. "It's our honeymoon. We have plenty of time to eat."

When he starts kissing me, breakfast is the last thing

on my mind.

* * *

We eventually go down to the hotel restaurant around nine o'clock for breakfast. It's an impressive spread offering everything anyone could want. I eat a giant stack of blueberry pancakes topped with whipped cream and warm maple syrup. Tyler settles for scrambled eggs and bacon—the man has no imagination.

"So now what?" he asks me while we're drinking our coffee. "What would you like to do?"

"I want to walk along the beach with my husband and enjoy the ocean view. Then I want to walk into town and see some of the sights."

We go back up to our room so I can grab my camera. There's no way I'm missing out on photographing this incredible scenery. Key West is gorgeous. It's like another world down here, like we've magically been transported to the Caribbean without ever leaving the US.

Outside the hotel, we stroll by the swimming pool, which is filled with men. All men. And some of them are taking the hotel up on their offer of clothing being optional. I keep glancing at Tyler, who's being careful not to look at any bare asses.

I nudge him with my elbow. "Are you blushing?"

"No!"

"Yes, you are. It's okay. You can look—just don't touch."

He glares at me. "As if I would."

Laughing, I slip my arm around his waist. "There's a lot of man candy here. I forgive you."

He surprises me by dropping a quick kiss on my lips— in public, no less! *Scandalous!*

"The only man candy I see is you, sunshine, so relax."

We pass the pool and head down to the beach. I'm wearing a pair of rainbow boardshorts with a white T-shirt. Tyler is wearing a pair of navy-blue shorts and an untucked, short-sleeve white button-down. He looks very *GQ*. We're both wearing sandals so we can easily take them off to walk barefoot in the surf.

I take scores of pictures of the beach, palm trees, the ocean as far as the eye can see, a bright blue sky with pristine white clouds. Everything's so perfect.

After spending a good long while on the beach, we head inland and walk down iconic Duval Street to take in the sights. We pass bars, restaurants, hotels, and a lot of tourist shops. We've been walking for hours and we've already worked up an appetite, so we stop at a popular café for lunch and dine outside on their patio, surrounded by potted trees and urns filled with tropical flowers and ferns.

We both opt for seafood, as it's bound to be fresh, and we'd be crazy to pass up on that. And we wash our food down with a local brand of hard lemonade.

As we relax after lunch, I snap a few shots of Tyler looking handsome and sexy with his sunglasses on. "Detective, you take my breath away."

He smiles. "I'm not a detective."

"You'll always be my detective." After taking another photo of him, I lift my bottle of lemonade to his and offer a toast. "To married life."

Tyler nods as he takes a sip. "I'll drink to that."

The sound of laughter coming from the table behind us draws our attention. There's a couple enjoying their lunch with their young daughter. The child, who looks to be around two or three years old, has long, curly red hair, freckles, and big blue eyes. The daughter obviously gets her coloring from her mother, who's also a redhead. The father is a tall blond with a body built like a linebacker.

While the mother is cutting up the child's food, the father is entertaining the little girl with a small stuffed animal shaped like a dolphin.

"Would you look at her hair?" I ask, nodding behind us. "I would kill for hair like that."

Tyler glances back and nods. "Cute kid."

I smile. "Maybe Sam and Cooper will have a redhead one day. Wouldn't that be adorable?" I take a sip of my ice-cold drink. "I've been thinking a lot about kids lately." I reach across the tabletop to grasp his hand. "You'll be such a great dad."

"Are you sure I'm not too old?" Tyler looks skeptical. "I don't know if I have the energy or the patience to keep up with kids."

I laugh. "You're not *that* old. And I think you're pretty patient. I mean, you put up with me."

Tyler laughs. "So, how many kids do you envision us having?"

"Oh, I don't know. Not that many. Maybe half a dozen."

Tyler nearly chokes on his lemonade.

"As many as we want," I continue. "I grew up in a family with two kids, and I always wished we had more. That's something I envy about the McIntyres. There's a ton of them."

Tyler laughs. "And they're adding new ones all the

time. Let's start with one or two and play it by ear, okay?"

I wad up my napkin and toss it at him. "Fine. But as far as I'm concerned, the more kids the merrier."

After finishing our lunch, we stroll farther along Duval Street. I still can't get over the chickens wandering around freely in the streets. That's definitely not something you see in Chicago, or pretty much anywhere, really.

We stop in at a tourist shop, where I buy several Key West T-shirts and some souvenir magnets to bring home and put on our fridge.

It's late afternoon by the time we're walking back toward our hotel. Up ahead of us, a small cluster of people has gathered on the sidewalk outside of a T-shirt shop. A police car is parked at the curb, its lights flashing. Two uniformed officers are speaking to a distraught couple. The red-haired woman is sobbing, and the big blond man is gesticulating wildly with his hands.

I grab Tyler's arm. "That's the couple who sat behind us at lunch."

I look to Tyler for confirmation. He nods. "Something's wrong."

We slow as we listen to what the father is saying to the cops. "Kinsley was with us right in there," he says, pointing at the souvenir shop they're standing in front of. "One minute she was there, and the next she was gone. We've looked everywhere—in the shop, in all of the stores up and down the street. We looked in the alleys and behind the shops. She simply vanished."

A male officer asks questions and takes notes. The other one, a female, speaks into her radio, reporting a missing child.

Meanwhile, the child's mother can't stop crying. She collapses to her knees right there on the sidewalk, while everyone watches on in pity. The woman's husband pulls her onto her feet and holds her tightly in his arms.

Eventually, someone speaks up. "I saw a little red-haired girl about half an hour ago. Just a toddler about this big." The woman holds out her hand to indicate height. Then she points up the street. "She was walking with an older lady, heading north."

"Describe the woman," the female officer says.

"She was maybe in her late sixties or early seventies. Her long white hair was braided. I think she had on a denim skirt, a long-sleeve blouse. Oh, and a floppy straw hat."

The police ask the parents to forward them a photograph of their daughter so they can put out a public alert for the missing child.

I turn to Tyler. "We have to do something. We can at least help look for her."

Tyler nods. "Did you happen to get a good shot of the girl back at the restaurant when you were taking pictures?"

I turn on my camera and scroll through the photos I took this afternoon, until I get to the ones taken at the restaurant. The family was seated right behind us, so they're visible in several of the pictures I took. "Yeah. I have shots of the little girl."

I hand my camera to Tyler, and he scrolls through the images. He pauses at one of the images, his expression tightening.

"What is it?" I ask.

He shows me the shot that's got his interest. It's a photo of Tyler sipping his bottle of lemonade. In the background is the little girl seated with her parents. "What am I missing here?"

Tyler points at a white-haired woman standing in the background of the shot, half-hidden behind a potted tree. Then he flips through the next few photos, and in each one the woman is there, lurking in the background, her gaze on the child.

"Oh, my god," I say. "Was she stalking them?"

"I think we have our primary suspect," he says. "At the very least, she's a person of interest."

Tyler approaches the police and introduces himself. "Tyler Jamison, former homicide detective in Chicago. My husband took some photos at lunch today that happened to capture this couple and their daughter." He holds out my camera to show them one of the pics. "We might have a photo of a suspect."

The father grabs the camera and scrolls through the images. "Oh, my god." Blood drains from his face. "Do you think this woman might have taken Kinsley?"

The officer shows a photo of the white-haired suspect to the woman who claims she saw a little red-haired girl walking with an older woman. "Is this the woman you saw?"

The witness nods. "Yes, that's her. I'm sure of it."

"We'll need copies of those photos," the female officer tells us. "I'm Officer Layne," she says as she hands Tyler a business card. "Please e-mail these photos to us as quickly as possible. In the meanwhile, we'll put out an alert to watch for the woman and child."

I catch Tyler's attention. "We have to do something," I whisper.

Tyler hands his business card to the parents. "We're private investigators. We'll help search for your daughter."

"Thank you," the mother sobs. She reaches out and clasps Tyler's hand. "I can't thank you enough. Please help us find our daughter."

"We'll do our best," he replies.

Tyler exchanges phone numbers with the child's father. Then we set off for our hotel.

"I'll grab my gun, just in case," Tyler says as his long legs eat up the ground.

It's a good thirty-minute walk back to our hotel. Tyler changes into jeans and a blue button-down shirt that he leaves untucked so he can conceal his handgun in a waist holster.

I change out of my brightly-colored outfit into something more subtle so I don't stand out in a crowd. I end up wearing a pair of khaki shorts and a muted teal-gray T-shirt.

Before we leave, Tyler asks me to e-mail copies of images of both the child and the suspect to our phones so we can show them to people. We also e-mail copies to Officer Layne.

Tyler calls the main desk and asks for our car to be brought around. Then we head downstairs and wait for the valet.

"Now what?" I ask once we're in the car.

He pulls out his phone and stares at the screen. "Does she look like a tourist to you?"

He hands me his phone, and I study the image of the woman lurking at the sidewalk café. "Not really. She's not dressed like a woman on vacation. Her clothes look... old. Worn out. Her hair is unkempt, and her purse looks positively ancient."

Tyler nods. "I doubt she's staying at any of the hotels around here. She doesn't look like she has two nickels to rub together."

"So, we're looking for a local then."

"I think so."

24

Tyler Jamison

Resting my hand on Ian's shoulder, I lean in closer to get a better look at our person of interest. "Female, Caucasian, approximately late sixties. She looks to be average height, about five-five, give or take an inch, and average weight."

"That describes a lot of people," Ian says.

"Any other identifying details?"

Ian shakes his head as he studies one of the photos. "No, wait. There." He points to a brown handbag hanging on her arm. "That's a Coach bag, but it's in terrible condition."

I frown. "What's a coach bag?"

Ian rolls his eyes at me. "Fashion isn't your strong suit, is it?"

"Hardly."

"Interesting," Ian says. "She's wearing run-down clothing, but carrying a Coach bag." He zooms in on the image. "It looks like a knock-off to me. So, what's the plan?"

I frown. "What's a knock-off?"

He smirks. "A fake. A counterfeit product."

"How can you possibly tell it's a knock-off."

"Because the logo's not right." He shakes his head. "Don't worry about it."

We exit the hotel property and cruise along one of the main roads that lead to Duval Street. "My gut tells me she's a local, not a tourist. Get on your phone and find out where the public bus line runs."

"You think she took a bus?"

I shrug. "It's a possibility." I nod toward his phone. "Find out which bus stop route is closest to where the girl was last seen."

While Ian researches public transportation, I retrace

our steps back to the spot where the abduction took place. Key West has a public transit system, with bus stops located up and down the main roads, covering the island.

"There," Ian says, pointing to a bus stop just three blocks from the spot where the police questioned Kinsley's parents. "That's the closest stop."

"She could have grabbed the child and whisked her onto a bus within minutes. They would have been long gone before the police even arrived on the scene."

As a homicide detective, I worked an unfortunate number of child murder cases—those were always the most difficult cases for me. But this is my first missing child case. At least officially. This case hits a bit too close to home.

When I was just a rookie officer, Beth was abducted from our front yard. She was only six years old. It was thanks to an observant neighbor who saw the kidnapper's white work van with a plumbing company logo on the side that we were able to locate my sister within hours and before she was seriously harmed.

I can't help but think back to that horrific day. When I got the call at work, the ground fell out from under me. I couldn't make sense of what I was hearing. *Beth missing?*

Our little Beth?

Ian lays his hand on my thigh. "You okay?"

Mentally, I shake myself. "Yeah. This case is bringing back some bad memories, though."

He squeezes my leg. "You're thinking about Beth."

I nod, then I lay my hand on his. His hand is warm beneath mine, solid, and it centers me. My heart is racing, and I tell myself to calm down and focus on the case. This isn't about Beth. But it is about another child, and we need to find her before something bad happens. Every minute counts.

We trace the route of the public bus north through Key West, noting all the stops and their proximity to housing. We pass businesses along the main thoroughfare, then we see houses and hotels. Finally, we reach the more typical residential areas of Key West—single family homes, apartment complexes, and eventually more sketchy parts of town with long-neglected trailer parks and industrial buildings. We drive to the end of the bus line, then turn back and retrace our steps.

Surprisingly, we see few people on the street—certainly no white-haired woman with a red-haired child. I'm pretty sure we're not going to get lucky and spot Kinsley, with her notable hair, standing outside where anyone can see her.

"We're going to have to canvass the residential areas," I tell Ian. "We need to see if we can find someone who recognizes the suspect."

Our first stop is a run-down strip of four shops—a grocery store, a laundromat, a cigarette shop, and a beauty salon. We stop in the grocery store first and show the young man behind the sales counter the best image we have of the suspect.

"Do you recognize her?" I ask him after showing him my ID.

He shakes his head. "No, sorry."

I show him a picture of the child. "What about her?"

"Nope." Again, he shakes his head.

We try the laundromat, the tobacco shop, and the salon, getting the same results each time.

"Well, that was a bust," Ian says as we return to the Corvette.

"We need to keep asking around. If she lives around here, someone will recognize her. And from appearances, I'm guessing she lives in a low-income area."

"Why'd she take Kinsley?" Ian asks. "Who would do something like that?"

I sigh. "That's the big question. Obviously, no one in

their right mind would abduct a child."

"So, she's off her rocker?"

I nod. "I think that's a safe assumption. We need to keep canvassing these neighborhoods. If she is local, someone will recognize her."

We come to a small apartment complex and go knocking on doors, showing the suspect's photo to everyone we see. No one recognizes her.

We canvas more local businesses, to no avail.

"Maybe she's homeless," Ian suggests.

"I don't think so. It would be hard for her to hide a child under those circumstances. No, my money is on the fact that she has a home. Either an apartment or a trailer or perhaps a house."

We come across a distressed trailer park situated next to an automobile salvage yard. It looks like only about half of the lots are occupied now. Since no one's outside, we end up knocking on doors and speaking to anyone who's home. Again, nothing.

"This is like searching for a needle in a haystack," Ian says as we return to the car.

"That's police work for you. It's thorough, tedious, and time consuming. But this is how it gets done. We just have to hope we find Kinsley before it's too late."

On a whim, I pull in at a roadside collection of food trucks. We've been at this for hours, and we're hungry. Ian and I grab hot dogs and cold soft drinks.

After we eat our food, we visit each truck, show them the picture of the suspect, and ask if they recognize her.

"Do you recognize this woman?" he asks a young woman operating a taco truck.

The girl leans forward to peer down at Ian's phone screen. "Yeah. I've seen her before. That's Rodney Grimes's mother."

We both freeze, taken off guard. "Do you know her name?" Ian asks.

The girl shakes her head. "No. I rarely see her, but Rodney stops here almost daily. He lives with his mom. He takes care of her, I think. She's not all there, if you know what I mean."

My pulse is racing. Finally, we're getting somewhere. "Do you know where Rodney lives?"

She shakes her head. "No. But it can't be far from here. I see him drive by every day on his way to and from work." She points to her right out the window. "He lives somewhere down that way. But the Stor-n-Go where he works is that way." She points in the opposite direction. "Down off Maple Street. I think he's a maintenance man or something."

Back in the car, we drive south to Maple Street. According to GPS, the storage facility is just five minutes away.

The Stor-n-Go looks like it has seen better days. The office is in an industrial-looking office building made of cinder blocks surrounded by strip storage units made from concrete walls painted white. At least they were white about a decade ago. Now the walls are covered in algae.

Each individual storage unit is accessed by a faded red garage door secured with padlocks. The grounds are pretty barren—mostly asphalt, no greenery to speak of. Certainly no flowers or bushes. What might have once been flower beds are now gravel beds sporting waist-high weeds.

Ian wrinkles his nose. "The least they could do is pull the weeds."

"I take it you're not impressed."

"No." Ian opens his door and steps out of the vehicle. "Let's do this."

I follow Ian into the office, where we find an older guy with a thin, gray comb-over sitting at a counter reading a hotrod magazine.

He looks up when we enter the office. "Can I help you?" he says in a pained voice, as if the effort was too much.

"Yes, excuse me, sir," Ian says, his upbringing shining through. "We're looking for Rodney Grimes. We were told he works here."

The old man narrows his eyes suspiciously. "Who's asking?"

Ian pauses a moment, most likely taken aback by the man's question. He pulls his wallet from his back pocket and withdraws his business card. "Ian Jamison of Jamison Investigations." He tosses me a quick grin. "We'd like to ask you a few questions."

"Got a warrant?" the man asks.

"Um, no," Ian replies. He shoots a glance to me and whispers, "Do we need one?"

I shake my head. "Ask away."

"We just need to ask you a few questions," Ian repeats. "We won't take up much of your time."

The man sighs. "Yes, Rodney works here. No, he's not here right now. Is he in trouble again?"

"We're actually looking for his mother," Ian says.

The man lifts blood-shot eyes to us. "What do you want with that old bat?"

"We need to speak with her," Ian says. "It's important."

The man shakes his head, dismissing us. ""Don't waste your time. Regina don't take kindly to strangers."

"Mr.—" I look expectantly at him. I don't see a name tag anywhere.

"Evans."

"Mr. Evans," I say. "We need to speak to Mrs. Grimes in relation to a child abduction. You can either tell us where we can find her, or I'll call the police, and you can tell them. Actually, I'm going to do that anyway. Your cooperation in the next sixty seconds will have a big impact on what type of call I make."

Evans lays his magazine down on the counter and looks from me to Ian, and back to me. "You never said you were cops."

"We're not," I tell him. I'm quickly losing patience with this guy. "We're private investigators. But I assure you, the Key West Police Department is just as keen on the whereabouts of Regina Grimes as we are."

Evans shakes his head vigorously, causing his comb-over to bounce. "I ain't involved in anything criminal."

"I didn't say you were, Mr. Evans," I say. "Now, one more time, where can we find Regina Grimes?"

He points down the road. "Prescott Drive. She and

Rodney live in the trailer park at the end of the street. I don't know the number, but it's a light blue trailer with a white awning, held together with rust and duct tape. It's right next to a telephone pole."

"Thank you," I say.

We head back to the car. Ian pulls up directions to Prescott. It's ten minutes away, back in the other direction—north. Sure enough, we find an old trailer park at the end of the street. These trailers have certainly seen better days. Rust abounds, as do cars up on blocks, discarded bikes, and toys strewn across most of the lots. Some of the trailers are boarded up, undoubtedly condemned.

We zero in on a light blue trailer beside a telephone pole, just as Evans said. I park two lots away.

Ian reaches for his door handle. "Do we just walk right up and ring the bell?"

I check my weapon, then tuck it into my waist holster. "Yes. Time is of the essence. We need to find Kinsley."

We walk right up to the trailer in question. Evans was also right about the duct tape and rust. Clearly, Regina Grimes and her son are down on their luck. We step up onto a rickety wooden porch that may or may not support our weight, and I knock on an old aluminum screen door.

There's no answer.

So I knock again.

No matter how hard I try to separate this case from Beth's abduction, it's getting more and more difficult to dismiss the similarities. I did the same thing at the home of Beth's kidnapper. I knocked repeatedly on the door, and no one answered.

Out of the corner of my eye, I note movement through the front window—the shadow of an adult moving behind a dingy white curtain. "Someone's in there." I pound on the door with my fist. "Regina Grimes, open the door!"

After a long pause, the deadbolt turns, and then the chain lock slides free. A moment later, the old wood veneer door opens a crack. "What do you want?" the woman says.

"Are you Regina Grimes?" I ask. I can see enough of her through the crack to confirm her age and the white braid and denim skirt.

"Yes."

"We need to talk to you."

"About what?"

"About your whereabouts earlier this afternoon."

"What for?"

"Mrs. Grimes, you'll either have to open the door and talk to us, or we're calling the police. And you will talk to them."

She hesitates. "Are you cops?"

It bothers me that I can't say yes. "No, ma'am. I'm an investigator working a case. We just want a statement from you, that's all. We promise we won't take up much of your time."

Regina Grimes opens the door and unlocks the screen. "Make it quick. I'm busy."

We walk into a dimly-lit trailer. The air is stagnant and smells faintly of cigarette smoke and fried food. The curtains are drawn, letting little light inside the trailer. We're standing in a small living room and kitchen. The kitchen looks dated, but it appears tidy. There's a hallway to my left, which I presume leads to bedrooms and a bathroom.

I scan the room, my gaze landing on a collection of family photographs hanging on the wall. They're old photos, decades old. Mrs. Grimes was a much younger woman then. She's photographed with two young children—a boy about five years of age and a girl who looks to be around two or three years old.

The photos may be old and faded, but not so much that we can't tell the little girl in the photo has long, curly red hair. She looks just like Kinsley. I nudge Ian with my elbow and nod toward the photographs.

"Mind if we have a look around?" I ask her.

She frowns. "You said all you wanted was a statement."

"Right," Ian says. "My partner just needs to get your statement." He gives me a telling glance. Then, to our suspect, he says, "Do you mind if I use your restroom?" Ian chuckles. "Too much coffee today, you know?"

Her frown turns into a scowl as she glances down the hallway. "Make it quick. It's down the hall, first door on the right."

Ian gives her a friendly smile. "Thank you."

As he walks away, I mentally give him credit for quick thinking. Regina Grimes is suspicious, as she should be, and it's obvious she's not playing with a full deck or she never would have let us inside her home.

While Ian's off doing recognizance, I redirect the suspect's attention. "Your name is Regina Grimes?" I say, retrieving a small notebook from my back pocket and a pen.

She nods. "How do you know my name?"

"It's public record, ma'am. I looked it up on the

Internet."

"Oh." She nods.

"Is your son at home? Rodney?"

She glances down the hall where Ian disappeared, then back at me. "No."

"Do you know where he is?"

She shakes her head. "He didn't tell me nothin' about where he was goin'."

"Was he home earlier?"

She shakes her head. "I imagine he's at work."

"I see. So, Mrs. Grimes, can you tell me where you were this afternoon around one o'clock?"

"I was right here at home."

A lie. Ian has photographic evidence to prove it. "Did anyone see you here at home at that time?"

"No."

"And you weren't downtown Key West, near Duval Street earlier today?"

"No."

"Tyler!" Ian calls.

"Excuse me, ma'am," I say, following the sound of Ian's voice. He sounds concerned, but not panicked. That's a good sign.

I walk down the hallway with Regina Grimes dogging

my every step.

She grabs my arm and tries to pull me back to the living room. "You have to go now. I done gave you my statement already."

I find Ian standing in an open bedroom doorway, his hands on his hips, a purely dumbfounded expression on his face. As I approach, he nods into the room.

The bedroom is painted pink, and there's a single white canopy bed with a pink-and-white floral quilt. The bed is loaded up with stuffed animals. There's a child-sized play table with chairs in the room, along with a doll-sized highchair and stroller. The furnishings and toys look old, outdated.

As I peer into the room, I'm shocked to see little Kinsley sitting on the floor, digging through a basket of old toys. Thank god, she appears to be in fine physical shape. "Kinsley?"

The little girl glances up at me. Her eyes are red, and it's obvious she's been crying, but otherwise she seems unharmed.

Regina barges into the room, clearly agitated. "You two have to leave now. It's time for Stephanie's nap."

The front door opens and shuts with a loud clang. A deep voice yells, "Mom? Whose car is that outside?" A moment later, a burly forty-something-year-old man with a pot belly storms into the bedroom. "Mom, what—" He stops short at the sight of Kinsley, his expression morphing from confusion to horror. His gaze bounces from Ian to me to Regina Grimes. "Jesus, Mom. What the hell have you done?"

"I found your sister, Rodney," the woman says, smiling brightly. "I found Stephanie."

Rodney looks pained. "Oh, god." He turns to me. "Mom's delusional, but I never dreamed she could do something like this."

* * *

I call Officer Layne to tell her we located Kinsley, safe and sound, and give her our location.

"Thank god," she says. "I'll call her parents and tell them to meet us at the station. We're on our way."

Rodney paces the living room, running his hands through his hair, muttering to himself.

Mrs. Grimes is in the living room with us, clearly agitated. "You need to leave now," she keeps telling me. "I gave you a statement. Now you have to go."

Rodney Grimes leads his mother to an old tweed sofa

and sits her down. "Mom, what have you done? Where did you get that child?"

"Who, Stephanie? I found her and brought her home."

Rodney closes his eyes and sighs. "My little sister, Stephanie, went missing back in 1986," he tells us. "She was three years old at the time. She was never found." He points to the family portraits on the wall. "That's her there."

He doesn't bother to say the obvious—that Kinsley bears an uncanny resemblance to his sister.

"Mom was never the same after Stephanie went missing. She's been growing increasingly erratic and detached from reality over the past decade. But I never imagined she was capable of doing something like this."

I explain to the son how his mother spotted Kinsley with her family on Duval Street. She managed to snatch the child from under her parents' noses and sneak off with her.

Rodney shakes his head. "I'm so sorry about all of this. That girl's parents must be worried sick."

I nod. "That's an understatement."

"Do you think my mom will go to jail?" he asks.

"That's for the courts to decide. I suspect they'll do a psych evaluation first, to see if she's competent to face charges."

Ian and I stay until the cops arrive. Officer Layne handcuffs Regina and takes her out to the patrol car. A second female officer, Bauman, carries Kinsley to a separate patrol car and secures her in a child car seat.

We're the last to leave.

"We did it," Ian says with great satisfaction as we get in our car. "We found her."

I reach over and squeeze his hand. "We did indeed."

"I feel sorry for the son, though. Poor Rodney. He seems like a decent guy, and he obviously cares about his mother."

"I doubt it," I say. "I don't think she's mentally sound enough to stand trial. My guess is she'll end up in a psychiatric care facility."

ఌ 25

Ian Jamison

With Kinsley safely reunited with her parents, Tyler and I can finally relax and return to the task at hand—celebrating our marriage and enjoying our honeymoon. After dinner, we change into our swim trunks and head down to the pool. As the brochure says, clothing is optional, so I'm really curious to see how Tyler handles getting his first look at a naked man. One besides me, that is.

We drape our towels across two available lounge

chairs to stake our claim. Then we head over to the pool entry steps. The water is deliciously warm, in part because of the tropical sun overhead, but I also suspect it's heated.

I wade in until the water comes up to my hips. Tyler walks in behind me, taking his sweet time. I resist the urge to tug him in faster. Like the former cop he is, he's busy scanning the surroundings.

I study him as his gaze sweeps quickly past a few of the guys who aren't wearing swim trunks. Tyler's expression remains stoic, but I think I detect a bit of a blush.

I run my hands through the water. "It's heated. Nice."

He nods, but doesn't say anything. I think he's *processing.*

I'm dying to pull him into my arms, but I'm not entirely sure where he stands on public displays of affection, even when we're in a safe environment. He's come so far in a short period of time, and I don't want to ruin it by making him feel self-conscious.

"So, we did good work today, didn't we, detective?" I figure that's a safe topic. It's better than me asking him if I can climb him like a tree.

He nods, distracted as he scans the occupants of the pool. There are probably a dozen men in the pool with us, most of them paired off. There's a small group of four men clustered together, laughing and teasing each other, and a few singletons who are scoping out the area.

I want so badly to drift closer to him, to put my arms around him. To stake my claim. *Sorry, guys, but this hottie is all mine.*

Tyler finally directs his attention to me and returns to the topic at hand. "It was definitely a team effort. I must say, it's nice to be involved in the front end of an investigation. When I was working homicide cases, my job was to solve murders. Now I get a chance to prevent them. That's very rewarding."

"It must have been tough today—bringing back all those memories of Beth's abduction."

"It was." He sucks in a deep breath and lets it out. "We found Beth in time—before her kidnapper could do irreparable damage. I wasn't sure what the circumstances were in relation to Kinsley's abduction, whether she was in physical danger or not. Turns out she wasn't, thank god. We got lucky, Ian. The situation could have been very different."

"It wasn't luck, Tyler. It was skill. Your years on the police force gave us a tremendous advantage in finding her."

He nods, then his gaze is redirected to a couple hanging out at the edge of the pool, at the deep end. One of the guys is seated on the edge of the pool. His companion is in the water, resting between the first guys legs. They're being discreet, but it's pretty clear one guy is going down on the other.

I can tell the moment Tyler notices them. "Hey, if you're uncomfortable—"

"No." Tyler turns to face me and comes forward, close enough that he can put his hands on my waist. "I'm fine. This is fine."

"You don't look fine."

He frowns. "How am I supposed to look?"

I chuckle. "How about, like you're *not* about to have a heart attack?"

The foursome in the center of the pool starts rough-housing, dunking and climbing on one another. They're clearly having a good time.

"I'm sorry," Tyler says. "I'm not very good at this."

Another couple walks out of the hotel and heads for the pool. They're both wearing Speedos, with towels slung over their necks. They're both big guys, with hairy chests and legs. One of them dives straight into the center of the pool. The other walks in more sedately.

The first guy surfaces near us, rising out of the water and sluicing back his shaggy dark hair. "Hey. I saw you two come in yesterday. We arrived right after you. Having fun? I'm Darren, by the way. My better half over there is Steve."

I nod. "It's gorgeous here. We've been busy, though, and we're just now having time to relax and enjoy it."

Steve joins Darren and throws an arm around his partner's shoulders. "It's heated. Nice." Then to Darren, he says, "Making friends?" He gives us a smile. "Darren's the outgoing one. He makes extroverts look bashful, don'cha, babe?" And then he kisses Darren's cheek.

Darren splashes his partner. "Stop it. I do not."

"I'm Ian," I say, moving next to Tyler. "This is my new husband, Tyler."

Darren's eyes widen. "Honeymooners, then?"

I nod. "Yep."

"Congratulations. So, where are you guys from?" Steve asks.

"Chicago," Tyler says.

"We're from LA," Steve says. "I'm a financial advisor." He nods to his partner. "That's how I met Darren. He's a client."

"We're private investigators," I say, feeling pretty

damn proud of that fact. "We're partners, in fact."

"In more ways than one?" Steve asks, winking.

"We're in room two-eleven," Darren says. "Ring us up if you want to have dinner sometime."

"Will do," Tyler says.

As Steve and Darren swim toward the deep end of the pool, I slip my arm around Tyler's waist. "Aw, you just made your first gay friends. I'm so proud of you."

"They're not my first," he argues. "Don't forget Cooper and Sam. And what about Chris and Trey? I have lots of gay friends."

I laugh. "Sorry, but Chris and Trey don't count. They're my friends. But I'll give you Cooper and Sam."

Without warning, Tyler clamps his hands on my shoulders and pushes me under the water.

I surge back up, sputtering as I catch my breath. "You did not just dunk me!"

He smirks. "I'm pretty sure I did."

"Oh, you're in trouble now, buster." As I stalk him through the water, he walks backward, keeping just out of reach. The water's quickly getting deeper, so movement is getting more and more difficult.

Suddenly, Tyler turns and dives beneath the surface of the water. He swims the entire length of the pool, coming up at the deep end. I take off in his direction, surprised by this playful side of him. It's not something I see often.

When I reach the far side of the pool, he's already out of the water, sitting on the wall. I swim up between his legs and prop my arms on his thighs. Impulsively, I push up out of the water and place a quick kiss on his lips.

He smiles. "Are you having fun?" he asks as he tucks wet hair behind my right ear.

I nod. "Are you?"

"Yes."

"Let's go for a romantic moonlit stroll tonight along the beach."

"I'd love to."

The rest of the week is magical, just the two of us relaxing, soaking in the Jacuzzi or the pool, taking long walks along the beach. There's no more drama. No more catastrophes. No more cases. Kimi texts us to let us know we have a new case waiting for us when we return home—but it's nothing urgent.

We do all the touristy things that people do in Key West. We visit the famous Southern-most Point on the Continental USA—a must-see photo op. We return to see more of Duval Street and eat at popular restaurants.

We visit an art gallery and ride a tourist train that takes us all over the island. We make a point of having dinner at Jimmy Buffett's Margaritaville restaurant.

On Wednesday, we rent jet skis and race each other through the ocean waves. On Thursday, we charter a private boat for a lazy, day-long excursion around the island. On Friday, we take Darren and Steve up on their offer to have dinner, and we meet them at the hotel restaurant. Afterward, the four of us go clubbing in The Pink Triangle for drinks and dancing. Well, Darren and Steve dance. Tyler and I hold down the fort at our table.

"Come on," Tyler says, standing. He holds out his hand. "Let's dance."

"Really?" I'm sure my eyes are big as saucers. "You'll dance with me? Here?" I glance at the crowded dance floor.

He grabs my hand and leads me onto the floor. As he grips my hips firmly, I throw my arms around his neck and pull him close. He surprises the daylights out of me by kissing me. Right there. In public.

Holy shit.

I think I've died and gone to heaven.

"Who are you and what have you done with my straight-laced, grumpy detective?" I ask.

He smiles, then leans in for another quick kiss. "It is possible to teach an old dog new tricks, you know."

"You're not old."

He rolls his eyes. "Compared to you, I'm ancient."

I bury my fingers in his hair and tug on the strands. "You're perfect."

I follow his lead as we dance to a club favorite by Demi Lovato. That song segues into one by Ariana Grande and then another by Lizzo.

I'm so touched by the effort he's making on my account, I could cry. "Thank you."

Tyler's gaze locks on mine. "You don't need to thank me."

"You're doing this for me, not because you really want to."

"I'm your husband. I want you to be happy."

After several more songs, we're both winded and parched. I head back to our table while Tyler goes to the bar to order refills.

Not long after I sit, two guys sit down at our table. They're about my age, or maybe a bit younger, and they're both trashed.

The blue-eyed blond one smiles as he leans across the table, extending his hand. "Hey, beautiful. We saw you guys out on the dance floor." He nods toward the bar where Tyler's waiting to place our order. "Who's your sugar daddy?"

Tyler's back is to us, so he hasn't noticed we have company. I bite back a laugh. "He's my husband, not my sugar daddy."

"Oooh," the other guy says as he glances down at my ring finger. This one has chocolate brown hair that flops over his forehead and puppy dog eyes. "We were just wondering if you two might be interested in some company tonight?"

This time I can't refrain from laughing. "One, no. You've seen my husband, right? I don't need company. And two, obviously you've never met him or you wouldn't ask."

"It never hurts to ask," the blond says. He offers me his hand, but I don't take it. "I'm Dane, by the way. This is Parker."

"Making more friends?" Tyler asks in a deceptively friendly voice as he arrives back at our table. He sets our drinks down—a Cosmo for me and a bottle of a local brew for himself. Then he sits in the only available chair. He's stiff as a board, and his eyes are narrowed on the two strangers.

"We were just feeling your hubby out," Parker says. "We were wondering if you two would like to hang out later tonight. Maybe in our suite? You know… for some cocktails and such."

"No, thanks," Tyler says in a congenial voice.

"Are you sure?" Dane asks. "We know how to have a good time."

Tyler drops his friendly persona. "Get up and walk away," he says in a hard voice. "Now."

"Fine," the blond says, pouting as he pushes to his feet. "Your loss."

After they've gone, Tyler finally relaxes in his chair. "You are a magnet for trouble."

"Me? I was sitting here minding my own business."

He leans close. "Finish your drink so we can go. I've had enough socializing. I want you all to myself."

I smile as I sip my slightly-sweet, fruity cocktail. "They thought you were my sugar daddy."

Tyler rolls his eyes as he takes a swig of his beer. "That's funny. You're the one with the money."

* * *

Once we're back in our room, we take a long hot

shower together in the large walk-in shower, taking turns running soapy hands over every inch of each other's body. We towel dry, then fall exhausted into bed. It's not even midnight yet, but we're both tired. The busy week has taken its toll.

"Hey, sugar daddy," I say, smiling as I edge closer to him.

Tyler pulls me on top of him, then lifts his head to kiss me. "Hey, husband."

I settle on his lap, our erections nestled perfectly together. He threads his fingers through my hair and holds me for a kiss. Our bodies are warm from the shower. I rub my nose against his shoulder, loving the smell of his skin. He lifts his hips, rubbing himself against me, and we both groan.

Tyler reaches between us, grasping both of our cocks in one hand, and he strokes us. The friction is delicious. We're about the same size, the same length and girth. I sit up, straddling him, so I can watch, mesmerized by the sight.

I take over, gripping both of us in one hand. I rock against him, and he caresses my back, his hands sliding up to my shoulders and down to my ass, and then back again. He runs his blunt nails down my back, making my nerve endings sing.

We kiss, our breaths growing hot and heavy. Our bodies slide together in perfect rhythm, hardness against hardness, firm against firm. As pleasure takes us over, our groans deepen. My heart pounds, and I know his does, too.

Suddenly, he flips us, and I'm beneath him. He grasps my wrists and pins them to the bed as he rocks against me, rubbing his length against mine, driving us both higher and higher. As if we're perfectly in tune with each other, we come at the same time. Our groans and gasps mingle until they become inseparable.

Afterward, I lie limp as a noodle. Tyler cleans us both up, then turns out the light and crawls back into bed. He lies behind me, his arms tucked around my waist, and pulls me back against him.

As I'm falling asleep, reveling in the feel of his warm, steady breath on my shoulder, I start thinking about the future.

"I want a baby," I say.

Tyler kisses my shoulder. "You'd be a fantastic dad."

"So would you." I lay my arm over his and link our fingers together. "When we have a baby, I want you to be the biological father. I want us to have *your* baby, Tyler."

Tyler tightens his hold on me. "If that's what you want."

I angle my head back to kiss him. "It is."

"And someday I'd like a little curly-haired version of you."

I smile in the darkness. "I think we can manage that."

26

Tyler Jamison

The week is over way too quickly, and it's time to fly back to Chicago. Kimi and Jerry have been keeping us updated on what's been happening back in the office. I'm pleasantly surprised with how the private investigation venture is starting to take off. It's not that we need the money, because we don't. I still have a considerable nest egg in the bank from the proceeds from selling my condo. And, well, Ian's loaded. Money's not an issue. But I like knowing I can support myself as a self-employed private eye. I don't want to live off Ian's money forever.

We pack up our stuff and drive to the airport, where we return the rental car and wait for our flight back home. While we're waiting to board, we hang out in the airport coffee shop.

Ian's been texting with his sister all morning. Layla's excited because she and Jason have decided to live full-time at his apartment instead of bouncing back and forth between his place and her parents' house. I'm sure that decision is bittersweet for Ruth and Martin. While they encourage their daughter to be independent, it's got to be difficult for them to imagine her moving out for good.

Of course she won't be completely on her own. She'll be living with Jason, who is dedicated to safeguarding both her physical and mental health. And Jason won't let anything bad happen to Layla. She seems really happy with him, and that's all that matters. And the good thing is she'll be living just a couple of blocks from us.

When our flight arrives at O'Hare, just before eleven p.m., Jerry is there with his SUV to pick us up and drive us home. "Welcome home, guys. I hope you had a wonderful trip."

"We did," Ian says, grinning at me. "We ended up solving a case while we were there. A young girl went missing when she was out shopping with her parents. We managed to track her down within a few hours."

"That's horrible," Jerry says. "I hope she's okay."

"Fortunately, she's fine," I say. "It was a case of mistaken identity."

Ian jabs me with his elbow. "That's one way to put it."

When we arrive at the townhouse, Jerry helps us unload our luggage.

"Thanks for the ride, Jerry," Ian says.

"You're welcome. I'll see you both in the morning. Kimi can bring you up to speed on what you've missed. You received several calls from potential clients while you were gone."

Ian unlocks the front door, walks in, and disarms the security system. I carry in our suitcases and carry-on bags.

Ian grabs the carry-ons. "I'll run these upstairs."

"I'll bring up the suitcases just as soon as I put my gun away."

Ian dashes up the stairs. As I'm securing my gun in the front closet, there's a knock at the door. I figure it's Jerry. When I open the door, my heart jumps up into my throat. It's not Jerry. It's Brad Turner, and he's pointing a

9mm at my head.

My first thought is for Ian's safety. He's upstairs, and that buys me at least a few seconds to wrest the gun away from Turner.

"I called your office today," he says casually. "Your assistant told me you'd be getting back into town tonight. I've been waiting for hours, parked right across the street." He smirks. "You drove right past me as you pulled in just now and didn't even notice."

I steel myself as anger threatens to choke me. "If you think for one second I'll let you hurt Ian, you're even crazier than I thought."

He laughs. "You idiot. It's not Ian I want to hurt."

As Brad steps forward, I step back. Once he's over the threshold, he closes the door behind him and locks it.

"You have a funny way of showing it." I force myself to remain calm. I'm no good to Ian if I can't get the upper hand here.

Brad waves the gun in my face. "No, asshole. I want to hurt *you*, you sanctimonious bastard. You act like you're God's gift to mankind. Ian doesn't need you. He can do so much better."

I scoff. "With you, you mean?" I strike out then, intending to knock the gun from Turner's hand, or at least avert his aim, but his index finger is right over the feather-light trigger, and the gun goes off.

My ears ring as I'm thrown back as fire tears through my right shoulder. I hit the floor hard, and my vision starts to waver.

God damn it.

A million thoughts flash through my brain.

I'm bleeding, bad.

Ian heard that shot. He'll be down here any second.

Turner stands over me, his face screwed up in anger. He points the muzzle of his gun at my forehead, and all I can think about is Ian and how badly this will hurt him.

Turner grits his teeth as he spews out his words. "You think so highly of yourself, don't you? You big shot Chicago homicide detective. You get off on harassing innocent civilians, don't you? Well, who's got the upper hand now, huh? Who's in charge? I am. That's who. I'm done with you standing in my way."

Suddenly, someone's pounding on the front door. "Tyler! Ian! Open up." It's Jerry, who lives just across the driveway above our offices. Of course he heard that shot. I imagine half the neighborhood did.

All I can think about is Ian. I can't bear for him to be the one to discover my body. It'll break his heart.

At the sound of footsteps racing down the stairs behind me, Turner glances up. His eyes widen in disbelief.

And then I hear gunshot, the noise deafening. It's followed by two more shots in rapid succession. My entire body flinches on reflex, sending a fresh wave of burning pain through me.

And as I'm struggling to stay conscious, I stare at the blood welling out of the ragged hole in Turner's chest.

My god, Ian shot him.

Eyes wide open in shock, Brad Turner topples backward, and his gun crashes to the floor.

Ian kicks Turner's gun out of reach before he drops down beside me and lays down his weapon. "Tyler." His voice is little more than a hoarse gasp as he lays his hands on my chest. "It's okay, babe. Hang on."

I hear him rattling off information, and it takes me a minute to realize he's on the phone with nine-one-one. His voice wavers in and out, and suddenly my limbs start to go numb.

Someone's still pounding on the front door.

I reach for Ian's hand and squeeze it weakly. "I'm so sorry, baby."

"Don't say that," Ian says. He releases my hand and runs to unlock the front door.

Jerry barges in and comes to a standstill when he sees me lying on the floor. Then he stares at Turner's lifeless body and the splatters of blood on the floor and walls. "Holy shit."

Ian takes my hand again while talking on the phone. "Yes, I'm still here. Hurry. He's bleeding badly. Yes, his shoulder. No, the shooter's dead. There was just one."

My fault," I mutter. "Should have been more careful."

"Shh." Ian bends over me and presses his lips to my forehead. "Don't talk. You're going to be fine."

Jerry whips off his T-shirt, wads it up, and presses it to my shoulder, sending streaks of white-hot pain shooting through me. "Hang in there, Tyler. Help is on the way."

My mind is starting to float. Ian's talking, but I can't make any sense of what he's saying. "Ian." His name comes out like a drunken slur.

"It's okay, baby. I'm right here. Just hang on. They're coming."

"I love you. Beth and my mom. Luke and Ava. Tell them."

"You can tell them yourself when they visit you at the hospital. Now stop talking like that."

I reach for my shoulder, but Ian blocks my hand. "Lie still," he says.

Hot wetness soaks my shirt. "It's bad."

"No, it's just a flesh wound."

He's lying.

I'm cold all over, and I can't stop shaking. "Ian."

He releases my hand to stroke my forehead. "Please save your strength, okay? You're going to need it. I need you to get better for me."

"I'm—" It's getting harder to form words. Harder to focus. To stay awake. "—sorry."

Ian presses his lips to my forehead. "Just rest."

"Doesn't... hurt... anymore."

The last thing I'm aware of is the distant wail of sirens. I'm just afraid it's too late.

ॐ **27**

Ian Jamison

J ust as Tyler passes out, I hear emergency vehicles pulling up outside our house. Thank god. It feels like it's taken them forever to get here, when in reality it's only been minutes. The front rooms are illuminated by flashing, colorful lights.

The pool of blood beneath Tyler is spreading quickly, and I'm terrified he's going to bleed out. Jerry and I make eye contact, and his stricken gaze tells me he fears the same thing. Jerry's putting good pressure on the wound, but that might not be enough to stop the bleeding.

"Do you think the bullet went all the way through?" I ask. If the bullet went all the way through, then Tyler's bleeding from the exit wound as well.

Jerry tries to peer beneath Tyler's shoulder. "We could turn him to look."

I think we're both afraid to move him.

Multiple vehicle doors open and slam shut. A moment later, there's a sharp knock on the front door. "Police!"

"It's unlocked," I yell.

The door opens. Two male officers storm inside, guns drawn.

One of them quickly checks Brad for a pulse. "He's dead."

"Is there anyone else?" his partner asks as he peers into both of the front rooms.

"No," I say. "It was just him."

Two paramedics come inside—a man and a woman—both carrying medical bags. They drop to their knees, one on each side of Tyler, displacing me and Jerry. Immediately, the male cuts open Tyler's shirt, and the female grabs supplies from her bag and starts packing the wound with gauze. When she's done, she bandages the area.

"He passed out about two minutes ago," I say, my voice shaky as I watch the female medic search Tyler's body for additional injuries. My pulse is racing, but I try to remain calm for Tyler's sake. He needs me strong, not falling apart.

The male medic, a young African-American man, runs outside and returns quickly to lay a board on the floor beside Tyler. After securing a brace around his neck, the medics roll Tyler onto his side, slide the board beneath him, and secure him in place with straps.

The young man rushes out again and returns a moment later, bringing in a gurney. Jerry helps them transfer Tyler onto the gurney, and they wheel him out the front door.

I follow closely, my heart pounding as I watch them carefully navigate the front steps. Once they reach the driveway, they rush Tyler into the ambulance.

Outside, it's utter chaos, with police cars and a firetruck blocking the street. The ambulance is parked in our driveway. Neighbors stand around in their pajamas, in small groups on the sidewalk, watching.

I stand aside as the medics load the gurney into the back of the ambulance. "I'm coming with you to the hospital," I say, looking from the woman to the man.

"Please."

The male EMT studies me a second. "As long as you do as I say and remain calm, you can ride up front with me. Otherwise, no."

I nod, not trusting myself to speak. I don't want to give them any reason to refuse me.

The woman climbs in back with Tyler, and the man secures the back doors. When he heads for the driver's door, and I rush around to the other side, slip into the front passenger seat, and buckle my seatbelt.

As the ambulance pulls away, I glance out the window and spot Jerry standing on the front stoop, his hands on his hips. He'll lock up the house when the authorities are gone.

I suppose they're waiting for the coroner to arrive and collect Brad's body.

I killed a man.

I shot him point blank.

I should probably feel bad about killing Brad, but I don't. All I care about is Tyler.

With shaking hands, I pull out my phone and call Sam.

"Hey, Ian," he says eagerly as he takes my call. "Are you guys home yet? How was your trip?"

"Yeah, we're home." My voice breaks on the last word.

Home. Tyler is my home. I thought I could do this and remain stoic, but I'm failing miserably.

"Ian, what's wrong?" Sam says sharply.

"Tyler's been shot. We're on our way to the hospital now. Can you let Beth know? And Ingrid. Someone's got to pick up Ingrid and bring her to the hospital. She shouldn't drive herself. She'll be too upset."

Sam's running now, panting. He speaks to Cooper in a hushed voice.

Suddenly Cooper comes on the line. "Everything's going to be all right, Ian," he says in a calm, steady voice. "You focus on Tyler and leave the rest to us. We'll take care of notifying his family. Yours, too."

My throat is so tight I can barely speak. "Thank you."

"Tyler's going to be fine, Ian," Cooper says. "I've never met a stronger son of a bitch in my life. There's no way in hell he's leaving you."

Tears stream down my cheeks as I stare straight ahead at the black pavement. It's pitch black outside, and we have only the streetlights to light our way.

I turn to look into the back of the ambulance. There's only a small window between the cab and the back. It's partially open, but I can't see much.

"We were married a week ago," I say.

The driver spares me a reassuring smile. "Then he has a lot to live for, doesn't he?"

I turn back once more, just as the medic hangs a bag of clear fluid on an IV pole.

"BP seventy over forty," she calls out urgently. "Can we step on it, please?"

I'm no medical professional, but that number seems really low to me. I can only see a small portion of Tyler's profile, but it's enough for me to see how pale he is. My god, how much blood has he lost?

"Don't you dare leave me, babe," I whisper. "There's so much we haven't done yet. So much we have to live for."

I listen numbly as the medic in back shouts out numbers and medical terms so fast I can't make heads or tails out of any of it.

I don't think I've ever been so scared in my life.

* * *

As bad as the ambulance ride was, it's even worse once we reach the hospital. As soon as we pull up to the emergency entrance, the medics whisk Tyler into the hospital through a designated door. I follow him inside, and a harried woman with a clipboard ushers me into a small private room. She sits me down and peppers me with questions, asking everything from Tyler's name and address, to his birthdate, medical history, and insurance.

"What's your relationship to the patient?" she asks.

"He's my husband."

"Does he have any preexisting medical conditions?"

I shake my head. "None that I'm aware of."

"Does he take any medication?"

"No."

"Is he allergic to anything?"

"I don't think so," I say woodenly, realizing how little I know about Tyler's medical history. "He's never mentioned anything. I could call his mother. She might know."

She documents everything I tell her. "That's all right. We'll check his online charts."

She leaves me then, and I sit alone in a very quiet room, waiting for news.

Sometime later—I've lost track of the time—a different woman wearing scrubs comes to tell me that Tyler is being prepped for surgery. She says something about an artery and blood loss. His clavicle is broken. And there's something wrong with his shoulder.

My mind is spinning, and everything she says jumbles

together. "Is he going to be all right?" That's really what I need to know.

She smiles gently. "He's in good hands, honey. Have faith. Now, if you'll come with me, I'll show you to the surgery waiting room."

I stand and follow her out the door and down a series of hallways.

A few minutes later, she ushers me into a crowded waiting room. "Wait here," she says. "Someone will come give you an update as soon as we know more."

"Ian!"

I turn to see Sam and Cooper walking toward me. Thank god, I don't have to wait alone.

Sam wraps me in a bear hug. "Any word yet? How is he?"

"I don't know. They're getting him ready for surgery."

Cooper comes forward. "Come sit down before you fall. Shane and Beth are on their way. Jake is bringing Ingrid. I spoke to your dad. He's bringing your mom. Jason and Layla are on their way. They'll all be here soon."

I nod, grateful. "Thank you." My blood runs cold. "I don't know if—" I stop midsentence, unable to speak the words.

Cooper pulls me into his arms and holds me close,

his arms like iron bands. "He's going to be okay, Ian. You have to believe that."

He's right.

I have to believe that because nothing else is acceptable.

More family starts arriving. Beth and Shane. Ingrid. Layla and Jason. My parents. We all sit clustered together in the corner of the waiting room.

Finally, a nurse comes to the waiting room with an update. "He's in surgery now. His condition is critical, but he's stable. They're giving him blood now."

My parents sit down, one on each side of me. My mom looks pale, and her usually neat bun is starting to fall, a few auburn strands dangling down her cheeks. They were probably about to get ready for bed when they got the call.

More McIntyres start arriving, as if once word got out, they started rallying the troops. Jerry and Kimi arrive. Kimi's eyes are red from crying.

Feeling utterly useless, I press my face into my mom's shoulder.

Sometime later—I have no idea how much time has passed—a nurse comes to the waiting room. I jump to my feet and meet her halfway.

"He did well," she tells me with a pleased smile. "His

vitals are stable. They'll be wrapping up soon and moving him into recovery."

"Can I see him?" I ask.

She nods. "Once we get him settled in recovery, someone will come get you. You can sit with him while we wait for him to wake up."

Beth walks up and puts her arm around me.

"I should be with him," I say.

She nods. "He'd want that. He's going to be all right, Ian."

Ingrid joins us. "Don't worry, darling," she says, gently brushing back my hair. "My son is strong. He's a fighter."

Beth returns to sit beside her husband. I return to my seat. Layla's seated on the other side of my mom, Jason next to her. His arms are wrapped tightly around my sister, who looks devastated.

Sam brings me a cup of coffee. "Drink this. It's going to be a long night. You'll need the caffeine."

Blindly, I take the cup from him. "Thanks."

The rest of the evening and into the early morning is a total blur. People come and go, some of them stopping to offer me words of support and encouragement, but none of it really sinks in. I just smile and thank them for coming.

Finally, someone comes to the waiting room. "For Tyler Jamison?"

I jump to my feet. "How is he?"

She smiles. "He's out of surgery and in recovery. He's not awake yet, but you can see him."

"Oh, thank god," I say as my knees threaten to give out. It's only through sheer determination that I manage to stay on my feet. I follow the nurse down a long corridor to the recovery room.

She leads me to a bed half-hidden behind a privacy curtain. There, I find Tyler lying deathly pale and still. He's hooked up to a number of machines, and there's an IV in his arm.

"You can sit here with him," the nurse says, pointing to the guest chair beside the bed. "Once he wakes up, we'll move him to a private room."

"He's going to be okay? You're sure?"

She nods. "The surgeon removed the bullet and repaired the artery. His clavicle is broken, and there's considerable damage to his shoulder, but he should regain full use of it in time."

She leaves us then. I sit beside the bed and stare up at a bank of monitors. Machines beep quietly as digital lines go up and down, measuring his every heartbeat, his every breath.

Finally, I bring myself to look at him, afraid of what I'll see. His complexion is ashen, his lips pale. There are dark shadows beneath his eyes. I reach for his free hand, cupping it in mine, and bring it to my mouth to kiss. "Please wake up, babe. Please tell me you're going to be all right."

But there's no response.

I didn't really expect one. He lies so still it scares me. I glance up at the monitor again to assure myself his heart is still beating. His blood pressure is still a bit on the low side, but it's better than it was when he was in the ambulance. They're still giving him fluids.

His shoulder is bandaged, and his arm is in a sling, held close to his chest. I have no idea how much damage was done. I just hope none of it is permanent.

But at least he's alive.

I reach out to stroke his hair. "Don't worry. I'll take good care of you."

My gaze locks onto his face, and I watch for a sign that he's about to wake up. I need to see him open his eyes. I need to hear his voice. But he remains as still as a statue. Only the gentle rise and fall of his chest assures me he's still alive.

I resume stroking his hair. "You can't leave me. Not ever. I need you."

The minutes drag on, and I lose track of how much time has passed.

A nurse returns periodically to check on him. "He should wake up soon," she says.

I'm so exhausted I can hardly keep my eyes open. I lay my head down on the edge of the bed and rest my eyes.

Just for a moment.

The next thing I know, someone is gently stroking my hair. I straighten. "Tyler!"

He smiles weakly, and when he speaks, his voice sounds like gravel. "Are you okay?"

"Am *I* okay? Are you kidding me?" I can't take my eyes off him.

He's alive. And frankly, that's all that matters. "You almost died, Tyler." I didn't mean for that to sound accusatory, but it does.

He squeezes my hand. "I'm sorry, baby."

I cradle his hand in both of mine. "I've never been so scared in my life." And that's saying a lot. When I was little, my birth monster used to lock me in a dark room with no food or water for *hours*. At the time, I thought *that* was the worst thing that could happen to me. I was so wrong.

Tyler brushes his thumb over the back of my hand. "I should have protected you."

"Protected *me*? You're the one who got shot."

He winces, but whether from pain or remorse, I don't know. "Turner got the jump on me. I should have been more vigilant."

"Brad's dead. He'll never bother either one of us again."

Tyler tightens his grip on my hand. "Are you okay, Ian?"

I've been trying really hard not to think about what I did, but I suppose I'll have to deal with it sooner or later. "Am I going to get in trouble for shooting him?"

"No." Tyler groans as he shakes his head. "It was self-defense."

"You're sure?"

He nods. "Just don't make a habit of it, okay?"

"I won't. I don't regret what I did, not for a second. It was between you and Brad, and there was no choice. But, honestly, I don't want to touch a gun ever again."

Tyler smiles gently. "You don't have to, Ian. I'm sorry about what you went through, and I understand."

I stand and lean over him. I want to kiss him so badly, but I'm afraid of hurting him. "How's your shoulder?"

He glances down at the bandages. "I'm still in one piece. That's good."

I move in closer. "I really need to kiss you."

"I think you should."

"But I don't want to hurt you."

"You won't. Just be gentle." And then he winks at me.

That's when I know he's truly going to be okay. I gently brush my lips against his.

"You know what I was thinking about right before I passed out?" he asks.

"What?"

"That I couldn't die yet. I hadn't given you a baby when I promised I would."

My eyes tear up. "That's a promise I'm going to hold you to."

28

Tyler Jamison

Ian's clearly shaken by what happened. It's partly because he's worried about me, but I imagine it's also partly because he shot and killed a man. That's not an easy thing to come to terms with.

He's been parked in the chair beside my hospital bed for hours. It wasn't long after I woke from surgery that I was moved into a private room. Ian hasn't left my side since.

Family and friends have been streaming in and out

of my hospital room for the past day, not staying long, but checking in to say hi. Mom and Beth have been here for hours, though, coming and going from my room to make way for visitors. Ian's family has been here, too, the entire time.

"Please tell your family to go home and rest," I tell Ian. "They must be exhausted."

As soon as I say that, there's another quiet knock at my door.

"Come in," Ian says.

The door opens, and Shane pops his head in. "Hey, I'm glad to hear you'll survive."

Even though it hurts, I smile. "Gee, thanks."

Shane nods. "I'm taking Beth home. She's exhausted, and the kids need her. My parents will drive Ingrid home."

"Thanks."

The last to stop in to say goodbye are Cooper and Sam.

Cooper stands at the foot of my bed and gazes down at me. "You good?"

I nod. "Yeah. I'm good."

"No more theatrics, okay?" Cooper tilts his head toward Ian. "I don't think this one can take it."

"Hey!" Ian cries. "I think I handled my husband getting shot pretty well."

Sam pats Ian on the shoulder. "Like a champ."

Finally, after everyone has gone, Ian turns down the lights and climbs carefully into bed with me, lying on my good side.

Every little movement jars my shoulder, sending white-hot flashes of pain through me.

"Sorry," he says, wincing.

I reach for his hand and link our fingers together. "It's okay. I like having you in bed with me."

"Do you need anything?"

"Not right now. Eventually, I'm going to have to get up to pee. I'm not looking forward to that."

"I'll help you."

"I imagine you'll have to help me with a lot while I'm recuperating."

Ian leans close and kisses my temple. "I'll take good care of you."

* * *

I stayed in the hospital for four long days before I was finally released and able to come home. Once we arrive back at the townhouse, Ian puts me straight to bed, and he's been waiting on me hand and foot since then, even though I'm perfectly capable of standing on my own two feet. I can even walk to the bathroom on my own, although I've had to resort to wearing loose knit shorts with an elastic waistband just so I can pull my own damn pants down to take a piss.

The police have been here twice to interview us and take our statements. They assured Ian that he's not going to be charged for shooting Turner. It was a clear-cut case of self-defense.

"I told you," I say as he curls up beside me in bed. It's early evening, way too soon for sleep. "We can go downstairs and lie on the sofa," I suggest. "Maybe watch a movie and order a pizza." Ian loves pizza.

"We can do all that right here in bed." He reaches for the TV remote control. "You're staying right here. Now, what do you want to watch? It's your turn to pick."

"You pick." I've switched to the right side of the bed so Ian can sleep on my left side. That way he can cuddle close to me and lay his arm across my waist. I'm stuck lying on my back while my shoulder is healing, so our movements are definitely limited.

Ian lays his head on my good shoulder. "Let's watch something upbeat. How about a romcom? I've had enough trauma to last me a while."

We put on a comedy, but Ian doesn't even make it twenty minutes into the movie. He's out cold. I turn off the movie and lie with him, simply grateful for what we have—each other.

"I love you," I say, leaning over to kiss his forehead.

He murmurs something inaudible but doesn't stir.

It looks like my little ray of sunshine turned into a tiger with claws when the need arose.

Epilogue

Sometime in the future...
Tyler Jamison

I'm about to explode with excitement as I head to the hospital waiting room to collect our parents and bring them back to our suite. Under hospital rules, only two visitors are allowed in the room at a time, but we're going to bend those rules a little bit. I pause just inside the doorway and take in the four of them—Ian's parents, and my mom and Joe. They're seated together along the back wall in front of some windows.

As soon as they see me, they jump eagerly to their feet.

"Can we go in now?" my mom asks. She looks beautiful in a pale-yellow dress with a white lacey sweater. Her hair is pulled back into one long braid, and her blue eyes are alight with anticipation. I note with tremendous satisfaction how she automatically reaches for Joe's hand. I'm so happy for them—for my mom, who's amazing and deserves to be loved and appreciated, and for Joe, who's a good man and a great husband. He's also a mighty fine stepfather to both me and my sister.

When Joe slips his arm around my mom's waist, and she leans into him, my throat tightens. Good grief. Married life is turning me into a giant softie.

As I wave them forward, I'm smiling so hard I'm afraid my face might crack. "Yes, you can all come back with me."

I lead our parents back to our family suite, where Ian awaits. As we approach the room, I can almost feel their eagerness. I don't blame them one bit. I'm still reeling with disbelief. Even though we've been preparing for this day for a long time now, it never felt real. It was always just a distant dream. But it's not a dream. It's our new reality.

I open the door and step aside so our parents can file into the room ahead of me. They head straight for Ian, who's seated on the sofa. He looks up from the tiny bundle cradled in his arms and beams with joy. "Hey, guys. Look who I have."

"Oh, my goodness," Mom says as she covers her mouth with both hands. Her blue eyes fill with tears as she stares down at her brand-new granddaughter. "Look at that hair," she whispers in a voice filled with awe. Gently, she reaches out and skims her fingers gently through the baby's dark hair. "She has Tyler's hair." She glances up at me. "Have you settled on a name yet?"

Ian holds a bottle for the baby as she suckles hungrily. He gazes up at our parents and nods. There's so much emotion in his eyes that I choke up all over again. "Her name is Elizabeth Ruth Jamison. We're going to call her Lizzie, so there's no confusion."

Mom sighs. "Elizabeth."

I don't know who's touched more. My mom, because we've named our daughter after my sister, Beth, or Ian's mom, because the baby has her name, too.

"She's beautiful," Ruth whispers as she carefully sinks onto the sofa beside her son. She puts her arm around Ian's shoulder and leans in to kiss his cheek. "I'm so happy for you, honey." Then she looks up at me. "For both of you." Her eyes tear up. "I know you'll be wonderful parents."

A couple feet away, Martin and Joe peer down into a bassinet on a wheeled cart.

"And this little guy?" Martin asks. "What's his name?"

I join them, and we all gaze down at the sleeping baby boy. "His name is William Alexander Jamison. We're going to call him Will."

"Oh, Tyler," Mom cries softly. She rises to her feet and joins us beside the bassinet. Her lips tremble as she looks down at her grandson. "Your father would be honored."

My dad's name was William.

Joe puts his arm around my mom and draws her close.

Mom smiles up at him. "Oh, Joe, just look at them. They're so perfect."

"Indeed they are," he says in his deep voice. He kisses the top of her head. "Just like their grandma."

Ian rises to his feet and props Lizzie on his shoulder as he gently pats her back to elicit a burp. He and Ruth join us at the bassinette.

"They both have your hair, honey," my mom says. "And I'll bet they'll have your blue-green eyes as well."

Ian smiles. "I'm hoping they do."

"How's Faith doing?" Ruth asks.

Faith Andrews is our surrogate. She gave birth to the twins this morning, right here in Chicago. We were incredibly lucky to find a local surrogate, which meant we could attend some of her doctor appointments with her and watch her baby bump grow. Faith and her husband graciously allowed us to be at the ultrasound appointments so we could see our little blips on the screen and hear their tiny little heartbeats.

"She's doing really well," Ian says. "She'll probably go home tomorrow. After she's had time to recuperate, we're inviting her and her family over to our house to see the babies. We hope you'll all come as well."

"We wouldn't miss it for the world," Ingrid says.

Will stirs at that moment, his blue eyes fluttering open. He stretches and lets out a little cry.

"Can I pick him up?" Mom asks.

"Of course," Ian says.

Mom lifts our son and cradles him in the crook of her arm. She presses a gentle kiss to his forehead. "My goodness, I can't believe I have five grandkids now."

Ian laughs. "Hopefully, there will be more."

Lizzie has finished with her bottle by now, and after Ian manages to get her to burp, he hands her to Ruth.

The two grandmothers sit together on the sofa, side by side, cradling the babies on their laps, taking notes and comparing features. The two proud grandfathers look on fondly.

Ian slips his arm around my waist and leans into me with a sigh. We're both exhausted, as neither one of us has slept much in the past twenty-four hours. It seems like the babies are on alternate schedules, one of them awake at any given time. We're both too wired to sleep.

"When can you take them home?" Ruth asks.

"If everything looks good at their next check-up," Ian says, "we can take them home tomorrow." He leans his head on my shoulder. "You kept your promise and gave me your baby. Two babies, in fact. You're a very good husband."

I laugh. "I had the easy job, babe. Faith did all the hard work. She should get the credit."

* * *

Ian Jamison

I hear them coming down the hall before I see them. Tyler rounds the corner and walks into the kitchen with a crying baby cradled in each arm.

"Somebodies are hungry," Tyler says as he gazes down at the babies. "I hope those bottles are almost ready."

"They are," I say, glancing at the timer. I have two tiny bottles of formula in the bottle warmer. "Just two minutes to go."

Tyler glances down at my journal, which is lying open on the island counter. "Do we really need to keep track of each time they poop or pee?"

"Yes. We want to make sure their bodies are functioning correctly."

"Do we really need to track exactly how many ounces they drink at a time?" He skims the chart. "Wow. Lizzie has quite the appetite."

"Hey, do not appetite-shame our daughter. She can eat as much as she wants. She's a growing girl, and she gets hungry."

As Lizzie lets out a shrieking wail, Tyler winces. "Apparently, she gets hangry, too."

When the timer goes off on the bottle warmer, I remove the bottles, dry them with a clean towel, then test the temperature of the formula on my wrist. "Perfect."

Tyler hands Will over to me, and I offer our son his bottle. He clamps onto the nipple and starts sucking eagerly. After Tyler gets Lizzie's bottle into her mouth, we carry the babies into the living room and get cozy on the sofa. We sit side by side, our shoulders touching, and watch our babies eat.

Both of us alternate staring at our babies and at each other.

"Whoever thought this would be our lives?" I ask, feeling overwhelmed with gratitude. "Bottles and diapers and three a.m. feedings?"

Tyler chuckles. "Certainly not me."

I'm sitting on Tyler's left side, so I'm leaning into his good side. "How's your shoulder?"

He shrugs his right shoulder. "It's good."

Ever since the shooting, Tyler's right shoulder has been giving him fits on and off. He had physical therapy for months after the incident, and he did manage to regain his full range of motion, but still, sometimes his shoulder gets tight, and sometimes it aches. I think it'll always bother him to some extent, but certainly not enough to impede his job or his daily functions. And that's really important now that he has two kids to take care of.

I gently remove Will's bottle from his mouth and check to see that he's not getting any air bubbles. Immediately, he complains about the interruption, so I pop the nipple back into his mouth.

"Don't forget, babe," I tell Tyler. "Layla and Jason are

coming over for dinner tonight."

Tyler makes goo-goo eyes at Lizzie. "Do you want me to help with dinner?"

"Would you mind grilling some burgers? I'll make a salad and some side dishes."

"No problem." Tyler sets Lizzie's bottle down on the coffee table and carefully props her on his shoulder to burp her. She lets out an impressive belch. "That's my girl," he says proudly, and then he kisses her forehead.

* * *

That night, after our guests leave, we give the babies a bath and dress them in matching PJs—soft white sleepers with adorable little baby koala bears printed on them. We've started cuddling with them both on our bed right before we put them in their bassinettes to sleep. When I say *sleep*, I mean that figuratively. We're lucky if they sleep three hours before they wake up hungry.

We remodeled the bedroom next to ours into a nursery, but right now the babies are sleeping in our room. We placed two white wicker bassinettes at the foot of our bed to make it easy for us to get up with them in the night. Since there are two babies, and two of us, we figured it would be most efficient if we both get up with them to do the night feedings.

Right now, the babies are lying on their backs, between us on our bed. We both lie on our sides and pretty much stare at them in awe.

Tyler grins when Will reaches up and grasps his index finger. "He's got a strong grip."

Lizzie sucks loudly on her balled-up little fist, her eyelids starting to droop. "She's sleepy."

As the babies start to drift off to sleep, we lay them in their bassinettes. Even though it's not terribly late, we're both worn out and decide to get some sleep while we can. God knows we'll be up again in three or four hours to heat up formula.

Tyler and I permanently switched sides of the bed so that I can lay my head on his left shoulder—the good one. I rest my arm across his chest. "Oh, I forgot to tell you. The Porsche dealership called while you were in the shower. Our new SUV is in and ready for pick-up."

"What color did you decide to go with?"

"Gray. I thought it was an appropriate choice for a family man such as myself. I did splurge a bit and ordered the turbo. There's plenty of room for two car seats, two diaper bags, and a double stroller. We're all set for our first family outing—when they're old enough, that is."

"And where will we be going on our first family outing?"

"I was thinking the zoo, if the weather's warm enough. Or maybe the beach, if it's not too windy. We don't want them to catch colds or get earaches. What do you think?"

Tyler laughs as he hugs me. "I'm fine with whatever you want to do." He yawns. "Goodnight, daddy."

I smile. Tyler has started calling me *daddy*—meaning I'm a father now. Not in the other way, LOL. "Goodnight, papa."

I marvel at how wonderful my life has turned out, blessed with Tyler as my husband, and now our two babies. I feel such a deep sense of satisfaction and well-being. And it's all because I crossed paths with a tall, dark stranger in a bar. If I hadn't stopped him and said hi, if he hadn't met me again that same night on a pier at St. James Yacht Club, we wouldn't be where we are today.

I tighten my hold on Tyler, who's already half asleep. "I love you, babe."

He presses his lips to my forehead. "I love you, too."

* * *

Thank you for reading *Somebody to Cherish*. Tyler and

Ian are very near and dear to my heart, and watching their love bloom and deepen gives me tremendous joy. Thank you for sharing their journey with me.

* * *

If you'd like to sign up for my newsletter, download my free short stories, or locate my contact information, visit my website:
www.aprilwilsonauthor.com

* * *

For links to my growing list of audiobooks, visit my website:
www.aprilwilsonauthor.com/audiobooks

* * *

I interact daily with readers in my Facebook reader group (Author April Wilson's Reader Group) where I post frequent updates and share teasers.
Come join me!

Books by April Wilson

McIntyre Security Bodyguard Series:

Vulnerable

Fearless

Shane–a novella

Broken

Shattered

Imperfect

Ruined

Hostage

Redeemed

Marry Me–a novella

Snowbound–a novella

Regret

With This Ring–a novella

Collateral Damage

Special Delivery

McIntyre Security Bodyguard Series Box Sets:

Box Set 1

Box Set 2

Box Set 3

Box Set 4

McIntyre Security Protectors:
Finding Layla
Damaged Goods

McIntyre Search and Rescue:
Search and Rescue
Lost and Found

Tyler Jamison Novels:
Somebody to Love
Somebody to Hold
Somebody to Cherish

The British Billionaires Romance Series:
Charmed

* * *

Audiobooks by April Wilson

For links to my audiobooks, please visit my website:
www.aprilwilsonauthor.com/audiobooks

Made in the USA
Middletown, DE
25 June 2022

67768786R00198